# Accept ME

J.L. MAC

*Accept Me*
Copyright © 2014 J.L. Mac

Cover design by:
Robin Harper-Wicked By Design
https://www.facebook.com/WickedByDesignRobinHarper

Edited by:
Erin Roth-Wise Owl Editing
https://www.facebook.com/erinrotheditor

Formatted by:
Angela McLaurin-Fictional Formats
https://www.facebook.com/FictionalFormats

Images copyright
Used under license from Shutterstock-www.shutterstock.com

# Table of Contents

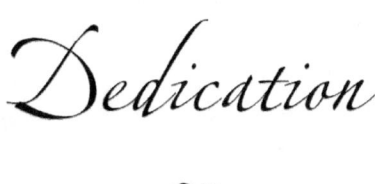

*Dedication*

---

*For Jo and Damon.*
*For what they represent.*
*For what we all dream of.*

# Acknowledgements

Where to begin? It's difficult to believe that over a year ago, while driving in holiday traffic, the story of Jo and Damon was born. In the span of a year, I became a bestseller, I made friends and lost a few, I was divorced and found love all over again, I moved, I laughed, I cried (a lot) but I was never alone through it all.

So many family, friends, bloggers, and readers have been on this crazy ride with me and I can't thank you all enough for your support, honestly, enthusiasm, and occasional bullying (I needed it).

First and foremost, I must thank my editor, Erin Roth. She has been the voice of reason when I was unreasonable. Thank you for working so hard, for seeing things through, for being pushy, for not accepting anything less than my best and for your brilliant editing ability. You are an invaluable asset to my books. I'd be lost without you.

https://www.facebook.com/erinrotheditor

I must sing the praises of my ultra-talented graphic designer and friend, Robin Harper. Your skill, insight, and taste with the covers of my books are unparalleled. I can't thank you enough for your hard work and kind words. I still have a lady crush on you.

https://www.facebook.com/WickedByDesignRobinHarper

To Christine Estevez, the queen of blog tours and cover reveals. You are the master of efficiency. I envy you. Thank you for working so hard and being so ready to take the reins every time it's cover reveal or touring time. I'll always put my books in your trust worthy hands to spread the word and promote. On behalf of all the authors you work with, thank you for everything.

https://www.facebook.com/ShhMomsReading

http://shhmomsreading.com/

Heather Halloran! My dear friend/blogger who teaches me a little more about resiliency every day. You have an exceptional eye for a good story and the guts to call out total shit. Thank you for being you and for the regular insults that make me smile even when I don't feel up to it. I love you, lady.

Angela McLaurin, my sweet southern friend and skilled formatter! Thank you for your exquisite talent for making my books pretty! You are the only formatter that I could ever trust my work to. You are the formatting fairy. I know I'm in good hands with you in my arsenal of book production pros. https://www.facebook.com/FictionalFormats

I must thank my agent, Marisa Corvisiero for her killer instincts and for having faith in my work. You have drive and ambition that most would envy. Thank you for working hard to make sure that the world may have the opportunity to stumble across my books. http://www.corvisieroagency.com/

As odd as it may seem, I must thank life for being so unpredictable and perfectly screwed up. It's only through failure that I learn to savor how sweet success truly is. Many thanks to my children, family and husband. You put up with my daily nonsense. There is no excuse for that except that you love me.

Finally, I want to thank my readers for reading the stories that I dream up. My characters come to life only through you.

# Prologue

---

## Beverly Wynona "Noni" Davis, January 17, 1979

I tried. I tried so hard. I thought he would be enough to distract me from my life and I thought I would be enough for him, but I was wrong. I was naïve. I guess I'm still naïve.

My parents would kill me if they had any idea what has become of me here in Las Vegas. When I told them that I dreamed of being a showgirl, they scolded me and said they wouldn't hear of it. To a working class Christian family, my aspirations were unthinkable—all those years of dance lessons and I wanted to become a showgirl when I could settle down and teach dance to five year olds in Podunk, Kansas? Ridiculous. It just wasn't what I wanted. In those showgirls, in that dancing, I saw nothing but glamour; I saw impressive-looking women with a real sense of confidence.

And I wanted to be one of them. I craved their expertise, their life. Staying on the farm would be the quickest way for me to end up leading an extraordinarily boring life as some farmer's wife. I'd likely have a few kids and end up not having a story to tell. I'd have no adventures to relive. I'd be sitting on my porch at eighty years old wondering why I didn't just go for it. I don't want to regret my life. I knew I had to go after my dream even if failure awaited me.

I never expected any of this. I had goals. I never expected Edward and I definitely never expected Damon. I never expected to be faced with this kind of decision.

I love him despite my circumstance. I loved him from the moment the nurse handed me my beautiful baby boy, but the darkness that he reminds me of is unbearable. I'm so very thankful for that he looks like my father, because if he looked anything like Edward I'm afraid I would despise him. I hate myself for even thinking it, but I'm not prepared to face what has happened. I'm not ready for this kind of responsibility. Not yet. Maybe not ever. It's one of the reasons that I know I have to do this. I have to give him a chance.

Edward's mother seems like a really nice woman. Beatrice. Even though I know very little about her, she's been so supportive of me in all of this. She made sure I had money in my pocket, food in my stomach, and a doctor to care for my unborn child. I never felt like she was judging me. She never asked questions and I never explained. She's been so willing to take care of me; I'm sure she'll take care of my son. I *know* she will love my child. There's no need for her to know how or why all of this has happened. I just need her to watch over him, protect him from the world, and watch him grow into what I hope will be a good man. A caring man. A man like my dad. I hope he won't hate me for letting him go. He doesn't have a chance in hell if I keep him. I'm just a stupid, ruined girl from Kansas. I'm damaged goods. I have nothing to offer my baby. Damon needs more than me. It will break my heart, but I happily accept whatever regret awaits me if it means he has the things that I can't provide.

I look down at the dark-haired angel in my arms and watch my tears splash down onto his blue cotton outfit. His tiny hand tightens around my finger and it's almost like he's consoling me. It only makes me sob even harder. "I'm so sorry," I whimper and lift him to place a kiss on his forehead. He may never understand, but I hope and pray that he can accept what I have to do.

Maybe someday I'll accept all of this too.

# Chapter One

---

## JO – REBUILD
## OCTOBER 2012

Months ago, on June 8th, I stared at my reflection in my tiny bathroom mirror, thinking about how shitty that day was going to be. The anniversary of my parents' death was like doomsday every year. If I had known that was the day I would meet the love of my life... *again*... I would have gone to work early and maybe taken more time doing my hair and makeup.

He poured into my life like the sunshine that followed him into the store that morning and I've been his ever since. I've been his the entire time, really, almost as if it was by design... like I was never even my own to give.

There was no falling in love with Damon. I was not swept off my feet and convinced to be his love. He came into my life, took my hand, and I *breathed* him. Loving him so completely is just a side effect of being so fiercely connected. It's involuntary. I didn't have to try to love him or imagine myself with him for the rest of my life. The moment he took my hand, it was clear; with just one look in those amber eyes, I knew I was where I was meant to be. At that very moment, I was his. Being Damon's didn't feel like a new adventure or some task. It was like coming home to a place I never knew was waiting for me. It was coming to grips with our connection that made my life change.

I'm not the type to believe in bullshit fairytales, but I do believe in what's tangible. I believe in what I can see and touch, and what I have with my Big Man is real. It's raw and so damn powerful that it took my miserable ass and shook me down to the frame, leaving me stripped and ready to rebuild. Four months ago, he came walking into my life and I had no idea what was ahead of me. Before Damon, I was alone in every sense of the word. We both went out on a limb to give our relationship a shot. Relationships were an unexplored frontier for me, but I was ready to map it out with Damon. Damaged or not, he was worth the risk. Given our respective histories filled with loss and disappointment, making a go of it was more difficult than I could have imagined.

My Big Man endured so much at the hands of a father who made his disdain for his own child no secret. Edward went out of his way to punish Damon at every turn. He drilled so many insults into Damon's head that he began to believe that he was responsible for a mother who gave him up, a car accident that wasn't really his fault, and my formative years spent homeless and struggling. My love has a way of focusing on all the negative parts of our past, whereas I just wish he could understand how much he's meant to me, how much he saved me.

It was Damon who recognized how important the bookstore was to me and Damon who saved the store that spared me from homelessness over seven years ago. He was there when I found Captain on his living room floor. He was there in the hospital when I said goodbye to the man who was like a father to me. Captain was a crotchety old bastard but he was mine and watching him slip away in that hospital bed destroyed the heart I didn't think I had. Damon stood watch as I mourned. While the initial burn of heartache has waned, I still ache for Captain, and Damon sees me through it. He always has.

Finding out that Damon has carried the burden of guilt all these years has only made my heart of stone a little softer. I don't believe that a man who has done so much for me and for Grams could possibly be responsible for the car accident that ruined four lives. The way he loves me and soothes the ache inside me, the way he thinks carefully about what's best for me and my future—all proof that he isn't capable of hurting me. I nearly lost him to a web of lies and blame, but I refuse to let him be the only one doing all the saving. He pulled me from that car but I pulled him from his own tangled wreckage of guilt. Edward was wrong. He never should have shifted the blame to Damon. I was wrong. I never should have walked away from him when I realized that my familiarity to him was because of our interlaced history. I should have allowed him to explain. I didn't and nearly losing him was the punishment I deserved. Enduring weeks upon weeks with Zombie Damon as my companion was difficult. I wanted to give up so many times but I just couldn't. I clung hard to the life preserver that was my stubborn will and it paid off. I brought him back from the prison of guilt that he locked himself in.

We've come a long way in a disarmingly short amount of time, but nothing has felt more right. I've never been happier than the day, three weeks ago, that he walked me through the house he intends on sharing with me. He stood there, in our new home, and asked me to be his wife. His wife! Forever! Seeing the inscription on the engagement ring drove it all home for me. *My heart resides with you.* Papa's inscription to Maman is elegantly scrawled inside the band of a ring that symbolizes so much promise for our future together. Damon knew how much that inscription would mean to me. He accepts me as I am. Flaws, painful reminders, and all, Damon accepts me for who and what I am. Merely his presence makes me want to be a better person. I've never wanted to be better so much. I've never wanted to fight my past, his past, and our fucked up connected past more than I do now. My motivation is tall, handsome, wounded, and he occupies my heart. A few minor things stand in the way of our perfect-screwed-up-life, but I readily accept whatever challenges lie ahead, because for me, there is no other option. Damon is it.

I walk with initiative into Grams' soon-to-be former residence with my cell phone pressed to my ear. Today is moving day and I'm not sure which one of us is more excited. I needed a few days to break Grams out of the old folks' home and get her settled in her private apartment at the new house Damon bought when he proposed (something I'm still kind of in shock about), so I delegated all responsibilities at the store to Noni. She seems to be eager to dive into the mountain of work waiting for her, but I'm still feeling a little anxious about it.

"Are you sure you've got this thing with the contractor taken care of?" I ask Noni as I hurry into the building.

"Yep. I've got it handled, honey. I'll take down notes for you," Noni promises.

"Okay, Noni, thanks for covering for me."

"No problem. I'll see you tomorrow?"

"Yeah, I'll be there tomorrow. And Noni?" I wave to Linda at the Welcome Desk while I wait a moment for Noni to respond. She knows what I'm going to say.

"Yes?"

"We can talk then if you want to," I say, doing my best to

encourage her to get through the talk that awaits us. I'm not thrilled with it, so I know she definitely isn't chomping at the bit to sit down and have the not-so-lovely chat about her past.

"Okay, Jo," Noni murmurs weakly.

It's obvious that this is tough for her and I'll admit that can't even imagine just *how* difficult it was to give up her child, but we still need to talk. Reliving the whole thing is going to take a lot of courage. She's obviously scared and she has every right to be. Shit got real in a hurry for all of us. Though I should be used to it—everything with me and Damon is a quick slap in the face from reality.

I swipe my thumb across the screen of my phone to end the call and then drop the beast into my bag, where it hits bottom probably somewhere between my lip gloss and Hemingway's leash.

As I speed walk down the corridor to her room, I glance at the new hardware on my finger. I've done it a thousand times a day since he proposed a week ago. It never gets old. My eye catches the glitter that the single gargantuan diamond puts off and it's as if I'm seeing it for the first time. A smile spreads across my face and my heart speeds with uninhibited delight. It's a welcome distraction from the *other* new development in my life.

Noni and I haven't had the opportunity to talk about the phone call that changed everything, even though we're both painfully aware that we need to. It's still difficult for me to believe that she—my Noni, my friend—is the woman who brought my Big Man into the world. Conveniently for both of us, work and moving have taken priority over that uncomfortable conversation. I'm dreading it. I think part of me feels like if I ignore this revelation well enough, it will just magically undo itself. Call it denial or ignorance or whatever you like, but the truth is, I'm afraid to learn anymore about Damon's sordid past. I'm afraid that knowing more will make me feel even guiltier for being dishonest with him and that's something that carries serious risk. My Big Man is on his way to emotional and mental healing after the disaster that our breakup precipitated. As crazy as it sounds, he's delicate at best right now. I won't risk his heart any further. The thought of him hating me for meddling is enough to make my stomach recoil. Silence is my oath. *For now.* Versan is going to have a fucking field day with this one. I'm not looking forward to that session. At all.

I'm walking so fast, my one track mind on my crazy life, that I nearly miss the familiar face standing a ways down the wide hall. *Edward.* He's the last person that I want to deal with today. The sight of him makes me sick and angry all at once. The pissed off part of me wants to run at him full speed with some type of medieval weapon, ready to pummel his head. A maul, maybe. Or a battle axe. It's a gruesome daydream, but it's the truth.

My pace slows as another familiar face comes into view. *Handy Andy?* And he's talking to Edward? Against my better judgment, I direct myself straight to them. Andy's eyes peer easily over Jackass McFuckstick's shoulder straight to me and he smiles that flirtatious grin that I've come to expect... and ignore. Edward goes on to finish what he's been saying to Andy without even acknowledging my presence. Damon made it clear to his father that he wasn't to interact with me in the least. As far as I can tell, he isn't testing Damon. It's a wise choice. I wouldn't want the full wrath of my Big Man raining down on me, either. It's yet another reason I'm beginning to regret knowing what I know.

"I've already taken care of it, Mr. Cole," Andy says.

Edward nods at Andy and turns to walk away. Just when I think he's going to heed Damon's warning to leave me be, he makes brief eye contact. "Josephine," he says calmly. His disposition seems indifferent, but something in that man's eyes makes my skin crawl.

I know I should refrain, but my mace-wielding inner self charges ahead. "McFuckstick," I greet him just as curtly as he greeted me. I can't help but rejoice a little on the inside. It's a small insult, but it feels good nonetheless. The very least he deserves is an insult or two. *Asshole.* I turn to Handy Andy, who is staring at me with a look of part amusement and part shock. "Trust me, he deserves it." I shrug and move the conversation into less irritating territory. "Looks like you won't have to make any more repairs to Grams' room after today."

"Yeah. I heard," Andy replies. "She's... interesting. I'll miss visiting with her."

We both laugh a little at his vague description of Grams. Interesting is a definite truth.

Grams comes into view right on cue, like a lifesaver from the sea of doom that stirs in the back of my mind. She's dressed in her favorite gear, a royal blue jogging suit paired with her usual brightly colored running shoes. It's such an impractical clothing choice given her age, but it matches her spirit to a T—she's bright and witty and full of energy. I love Grams and I make it no secret. Damon knows how close she and I have become over the course of my relationship with him. Moving her into our home means so much to me—I'm excited to have a real family again. I hated having to go to some retirement home just to see Grams. Having her so close will mean she's safe and taken care of by the two people who love her most. Most importantly, she'll be away from staff who have no vested interest in her happiness or well-being. They remind me of the caretakers in the orphanage; they do their job, but beyond that, I don't think they really care about Grams just like I don't think the caretakers at the orphanage really cared about me.

"Hey, gorgeous!" I coo upon entering her room.

She turns to me with a smile mirroring my own. It's a

sight that makes my heart swell to the bursting point.

"Hey! You come to break me outta here?" she teases.

"You got it. Looks like you're just about ready," I say, observing the neatly stacked moving boxes in the corner waiting to be picked up by the movers that Brian hired for the job. Handy Andy's work, no doubt. "I see Andy must've helped you a little?" I raise a brow with my little innuendo.

"Nuh-uh!" she scoffs, wagging a finger at me. "I don't kiss and tell."

We both laugh at our usual banter. It's another thing that never gets old. From the first time I met Grams I knew I would love her and thankfully, she must've thought the same, because our bond was instant. We shared a connection right away, just like I shared a connection with her handsome grandson. I knew when her blue eyes met mine that she was a safe place for me. She was witty, and full of life, and exactly what I needed, especially now that Captain is gone.

"What's Edward doing here?" I ask, peeking out into the hallway to see if he's still lurking around.

"Eddie hasn't visited me since I found out about Damon's journals. I haven't had the chance to ask him about the money either. I hope he had nothing to do with that mess but who knows?" Grams' mood turns grave and we both look to our feet, recalling the composition notebooks that uncovered the years of heinous abuse that Damon endured in silence. Grams hasn't said much to me about whether or not she has confronted Edward about the notebooks, but I imagine she has. I can't see Grams holding back after what she found out and she's definitely not the type to bite her tongue. It's yet another way that she and I are two birds of a feather. As for the missing money, I imagine her take on it is the same as mine—Damon is taking care of it. It's as simple as that. I know that in her heart she knows that Edward is likely at the center of the missing money, but he's her son and despite his destructive behavior, she probably hopes that the check fraud, for once, isn't his dirty work.

Damon knows that I told Grams' and Elise, his sister, about the abuse, but we never discussed the details. It's likely avoidance on both our parts. He and I have discussed the notebooks, but that's it. We haven't taken the time to talk about confronting the abuse as a family. I've tried to find the right time to tackle that issue, but it just hasn't come yet. Damon has endured one blow after another lately and I don't think I could put him through more. Not right now anyway. Thankfully, Elise and Grams' have agreed to keep quiet until I can smooth this over with him. Secrets aren't welcome in our relationship and yet I'm walking around with one that is capable of pulling the rug from beneath my Big Man. I'm no idiot. I know that when he finds out he'll be angry. I just hope he isn't as mad as I think he'll be.

"Oh," I reply quietly, patting her hand. "I just saw him in the hallway. I called him McFuckstick, so maybe he thought better of visiting." I smile recalling my insult, but Grams isn't amused.

"Jo, just leave him be, you understand? I've known that Eddie's a monster for a long time, but I'm his mother and I tried to see the best in him. Don't poke the sleeping dog, ya know what I mean?" She shakes her head, her face awash with disappointment.

I just nod in understanding and agreement to leave the asshole be. What's done is done and Damon and I are building a life together that has no room for that drunken fool.

Grams shuffles around the box at her feet and motions for me to follow her to the sitting area where we've spent so much time together. I follow obediently and watch as she takes on a serious demeanor as rare as a full eclipse. "Jo, I want you to be honest with me now. No joking." She caps off her statement with a pointed finger.

*Oh shit.* I nod and wait for it. She can't possibly know about Noni. No one knows. *Unless she's always known? There's no way. Is there?*

"I know you've said a thousand times how you want me at home with you and Damon, but I just need you to know that you don't have to do this."

I silently take a breath of relief that this has nothing to do with Noni. It's proof that my growing paranoia is an issue. I begin shaking my head in protest at her speech and start to open my mouth to speak.

"Sweetheart, I'm old and falling apart. I don't want to be a burden for you and Damon. I can stay here," she insists.

"Grams, you aren't *that* old! Hell, you're the youngest blue-hair I know." I reach across and pretend to ruffle her silver hair.

She bats my hand away and narrows her blue eyes at me. "Hey! I haven't let that beauty school crew touch my hair since that whole mess. It washed out just fine," she mumbles, patting her short silver curls. "I mean it, Jo. I'm old as the hills. I'm just fine with staying here."

"If you're old as the hills now, how old will you be next year?" I do my best to make light of the conversation that there really isn't a need for. She's coming home with us and that's final.

"Well, I'm old as the hills now, I'll be older than sin next year and older than dirt the year after that." She smiles a toothy grin that has us both erupting in laugher, as per usual.

"Come on. It's time for you to see your new home." I stand and lead Grams away from this place and to the home that awaits both of us.

The first home I've had since Maman and Papa died.

The home that Damon has made.

# Chapter Two

## COMPLETENESS

The entire ride to the new house is nerve wracking as hell. I want Grams to love the new place as much as I do. Anyone with a brain would be impressed with the property; I know that, but I can't help my rising anxiety. The house itself doesn't mean a damn thing if she doesn't feel at home here.

I peek over at her in the passenger seat of the pricey SUV that Damon insisted upon. She's been quiet and watchful of the passing scenery the entire drive, which is unlike Grams. Her silence magnifies my already sky high level of concern.

I carefully pull into the drive and switch off the ignition. "Ready?" I ask nervously.

"As I'll ever be," she chimes back right on cue.

I snatch her walker from the cargo net in the back and jog

around the car to help her out. She eases out of the passenger seat and onto her feet, a wide smile exposing her dentures. Those awful, giant, pearly white dentures! I've never been so pleased to see them in their full, toothy glory. *She likes it. Thank fuck!* I melt into a puddle of sweet reprieve nearly instantly.

"Niiice crib," she drawls out coolly.

My eyebrows arch skyward at her terminology. She's hilarious. "Crib, huh?" I mock.

"I keep up with the youngsters' language."

I don't doubt it for one second either. Cable TV has been her insight into the world from inside the retirement home. Her blue eyes light up and I turn to confirm what I already know has earned Grams' smile. That particular smile is reserved for only one person.

"Damon, you've really gone all out this time." She edges around me and heads for my Big Man, who is standing under the awning at the front entrance looking like heaven personified.

I've never seen a more gorgeous man. When my eyes land on him, whether it's the first time or the one thousandth time that day, it's like seeing him for the first time; my stomach flutters as I drink in every handsome attribute. His height. His frame, filled out with the perfect amount of lean muscle. His dark hair. His defined jaw, spattered with coarse five o'clock shadow that he knows I love. The sleeves of his dress shirt rolled up his forearms exposing ribbons of sinewy muscle. Of all things about Damon Cole that leave me breathless, his eyes are by far my favorite. Persuasive doesn't even adequately describe those golden irises of his. Those eyes are captivating. Absorbing. My gaze meets his and I'm sucked neck deep in an instant, like some strange gravitational pull so damn intense draws me nearer to him and is impossible to escape. Even if I felt like fighting, I wouldn't do any good because that same force that pulls me into Damon's orbit steals any desire for solitude that I once had. I'm his. And then there's that subtle smile when his eyes meet mine, that smile that's always laced with something more, something primal and compelling that consumes us both—one look in those eyes, one glance at that smile, and it's clear as crystal to both of us that I am exactly where I belong.

He doesn't even have to speak. Not aloud anyway. Something in the way he's looking at me sets my feet moving on a path straight to his arms.

"You were gone too long," he says just loud enough for me to hear.

I wrap my arms around his middle and rest my cheek against his chest. Grams is milling about on the front porch taking all of it in and I can't help but watch her and smile.

"I would say she likes it," I whisper to Damon.

His lips meet my hairline, where he plants a tender kiss. "I think you're right. Lunch is waiting for you two. Go eat."

Damon's phone buzzes from inside his pocket and he releases me to answer it. I turn and watch Grams, who is carefully cataloguing the front of the house, muttering to herself about the paint color and the shutters.

"Tell me good news, Mike," Damon says into his cell phone as he disappears into the house.

*Who the hell is Mike?* Although I've never been introduced to or even heard of this Mike person he's talking to, it doesn't shock me that Damon has business with people that I don't even know of. He's got his hands in various pots of all shapes, sizes and profitability and that means business dealings with a multitude of people. I'm sure it's boring work crap and nothing exciting. I leave him to it and waste no more time getting Grams all settled in her brand new *crib*.

Four hours, a delicious lunch, one *Golden Girls* episode, and a bag of Circus Peanuts later, and Grams is moved in. Thanks to my thoughtful Big Man, getting her things put away took very little effort on our part. He had the apartment fully-furnished, including a wall of cherry wood shelving to fill with her knick-knacks, trinkets, and do-dads, and even had the bed already made with some obnoxiously floral bedding. Somehow Brian swooped in while we were eating lunch with all of her boxes from the home, leaving very little real "work" for me, just organizing all of her thingamajigs onto her new shelves and putting some clothes away. Two-thirds of our unpacking time was spent chatting and joking with each other. She told me all about her high school sweetheart and a whole host of other transgressions that I was sworn to secrecy about. Turns out, Grams has always been quite the little firecracker. Not that I'm surprised. She's a straight up vixen and I love her for it.

The remainder of my day passed easily. I helped Grams settle in and left her to get acquainted with her new place while I went over some plans for the store, not getting back over to her apartment to say goodnight until well after dinner. After a quick tour of all the reorganizing she did, I make my weary way upstairs to our new master suite to find Damon already showered and dressed, or shall I say *undressed,* for bed. He's lying across our mammoth bed in nothing but those yummy little trunk underwear. They hug and hold tight to every delicious curve of his... assets. The bulge of his considerable girth is evident even when he's relaxed and I can't help but lick my lips. The elastic fabric clings and cups him so perfectly that my fingers feel a little itchy. It's a hell of a sight that has my mouth watering for the salty velvet taste of him on my tongue.

I pause at the door and take a moment to breathe in the sight of him. He's watching me watch him and the air between us grows heady and thick all at once.

"Get over here. I need to be inside my future wife," he orders in a composed voice, ripe with the guarantee of pleasure.

Without saying a word, I stroll across the space between us. Damon sits upright and swings his legs off the side of the bed, inviting me to stand between his bare, beefy thighs. I do as he silently ordered. His hands envelope each of mine at my sides and drift slowly up my naked arms, coming to a halt at my neck. His fingers curl around the nape of my neck as the other hand cups my jaw. I'm pulled closer to him, our faces only millimeters apart. His heavy eyes slide shut. It's clear that my Big Man is doing what he does so frequently. He's savoring this. He's savoring me. He's taking his sweet time because more often than not, that's just how he prefers it. My lips are achingly close to his. As many times as I've felt the fullness of his mouth covering mine, it never gets old. I edge my head forward, hoping that my wanton lips can coax his perfect mouth into giving me what I long for. The grip he has on the nape of my neck tightens fractionally, keeping me in place. It keeps me deprived of what I want and only works to cultivate my appetite for all of him. Just as he wants me. Damon is a calculated man. He has a purpose and a plan for everything he does. Even in the bedroom. His hand on my neck is a subtle way to control and direct me. I happily accept his control over my body.

"You have to get this wedding planned," he says hoarsely. "I don't know how much longer I can wait to make you my wife."

Before I can respond to his confession, I'm hauled up in

his powerful arms. In one fluid movement, I'm on my back, still fully clothed except for my bare feet. Damon kneels between my widespread legs and flicks open the button and zipper of my denim shorts, tugging them down as I plant my heels and lift my ass. He grasps the waistband of both my shorts and panties and frees me of them, swiftly moving his attention to my cap-sleeved blouse. The soft fabric is lifted up my torso, exposing the beige lace bra that I chose to wear today. The shirt is carefully drawn up over my head then tossed to the floor somewhere beside our bed. It takes him all of a fraction of a second to relieve me of my bra. He falls forward, catching the weight of his body on one carefully planted palm. His other hand clasps me behind my knee, hoisting one leg up on his hip. Once he's got me spread wide and bare for him, he eyes me carefully. Something unspoken blazes bright in his amber eyes. It's unfamiliar and it sets me off balance as soon as I see it. He's got something to say but he isn't uttering a word. I could ask him what it is, but I know better. Damon isn't the type of man that can be coerced, bullied, bribed, or threatened into doing or saying *anything*. I hold my tongue, hoping he'll tell me without my having to pry.

After a lingering look, eye to eye, his lips part to speak. "You know how much I love you, right?"

I nod in response, tightening my leg around his hip and hoping he's about to tell me what's going on.

"And you know I would never let anything happen to you?" he says softly, forcefully, holding my gaze. "You know that no matter what, I'd do anything to keep you safe and happy?"

I nod, careful not to let the confusion show on my face. *Why is he saying this right now? Is there something going on that I don't know about?*

"Say it, Jo," he insists, still looking down at me.

"I know," I oblige him.

"Good," he whispers, his lips pressed to my neck.

My eyes automatically slide shut. My back arches into him so that my peaked nipples meet with the sculpted muscle of his burly chest. The light touch isn't nearly enough and it sends my need for him over the top. I use what little leverage I have to pull him to me. My leg tightens around his hip again, pulling him down to me. I can feel a smile spread across those masterful lips of his. A needy moan slips out. With practiced ease, he sinuously slips off his underwear. Damon has heard my plea. My eyes follow his hand to his extensive cock, where he grips himself, taking one drawn out stroke down then back up. With my heart hammering hard in my chest, my breathing comes in rapid shallow puffs. He directs the swollen tip of himself to my pulsing clit. The lightest touch has me squirming for him. I want him. I need him filling me. He looks at me once more, then allows his wide tip to slip down my slick opening and into position. I still myself and prepare for him. It's more than enough to distract me from the gravity of what I have to discuss with Noni tomorrow. His eyes bore into me as he lunges his length deep inside me, stealing my breath and replacing it with a sensation that only Damon Cole knows how to elicit from me. *Completeness.*

# Chapter Three

---∾---

## SHARED WEIGHT

The day has gone by in some weird *Stepford Wives* monotonous fashion. Noni has kept busy cleaning, organizing and reorganizing and I've used any and every excuse I could to stay in my office with Hemingway as my only company. She kept meticulous notes while I was out yesterday, and each little sticky note detailing every phone call and delivery is conveniently posted at my desk. I know Noni's efficient, but I'm sure her detailed note taking has everything to do with avoiding me. I know that this whole situation must be weighing on Noni the way it has been weighing on me, but I hate that I have to psyche myself up to talk to her. I hid out in the office for the majority of the day browsing listlessly through a wedding magazine that I picked up at the checkout counter in the grocery store. This hoity-toity wedding shit definitely isn't my style. We've been engaged for a mere three weeks and I'm already lost in Wedding World when I really should be focusing on the store. Various contractors, and venders have been in and out and back in again over the last month and some days it's enough to make my head spin. The grand reopening is quickly approaching and there's a mass of things yet to be done. One plus to hiding in my hole, avoiding Noni and the truth, is that I managed to get a huge amount of clerical crap done.

This situation with Noni is the most uncomfortable I think I've ever been. I'm trying to use kid gloves with her but I'm afraid to make a move. I'm nervous that I may say something wrong or insulting and she'll quit, leaving me to explain to Damon why my prize employee has bailed on me. And I like Noni—I feel like I've known her forever—so this bonus information scares the shit out of me. Especially because I have to keep it to myself.

I peek over at her every so often to see if she looks like she may be ready to sit down and talk, but so far—nothing. *Nothing. Nada. Zip. Zero. What the hell am I to do with that?* I shouldn't push her. I can't push her. *Right?* She's a busy little worker bee on a steady roll cleaning, organizing and stocking inventory. Under any other circumstance, her work ethic would be nothing to complain about, but right now it's just plain awkward. I know she's avoiding me and she's bound to know that I'm doing the same.

I roll my eyes at the mess I've put myself in and push back from my desk. Closing time has come already, leaving me wondering if we're going to talk at all today. And if we don't talk, will every day be like this? If this is what I have to look forward to, I don't think I'll be able to take it for very long. Something has got to give here. I can't keep walking around knowing what I know and have Noni pretending that I don't know. We need to talk. Soon. One of us has to speak up.

*Come on, Jo. Get your shit together.* I give myself a pushy pep talk while I head to the front of the store to lock up. Just as I flip the sign, I glance up at the familiar bell on the arm of the door and smile remembering the simple days when it was just me and Captain running the sinking ship that was Bookends. As bad as those days seemed, I do kind of miss them. Life was predictable then. Now, everything is beautifully terrible.

I have the love of my life who also happens to be the man whose father killed my parents.

I have Bookends but no Captain to eat cheap takeout with.

I have Noni working here, making some amazing things happen in the coffee bar, but an obstacle stands between us that could ruin everything.

If Captain were here, he would take the lead on this. I can

imagine him looking at me with that incredulous smirk and telling me to "toughen up, Miss America. Get your big girl panties on and take care of business." After which he would likely go on some rant about how this generation is comprised of primarily panty-waisted cream puffs who don't know the definition of hard work.

I miss him so.

Lost in my thoughts, I'm caught off guard when I nearly run into Noni on my way back to the office. "Oh, hey," I sputter, all tongue-tied.

Noni gives a tight smile then looks down to the towel in her hands. She's nervously working the cloth between her fingers, visibly struggling to speak. It's painful to watch.

*Grow a pair, Miss America!* I hear Captain's taunting words in my head and I couldn't agree with him more.

"Wanna come with?" I motion toward the office, inwardly bolstering my metaphorical pair.

Noni nods her head and follows me as I step around her and head back to my hidey hole. I tug Captain's rickety office chair over so that I'm sitting closer to Noni. She's placed herself in the only other seat in the small space. It's just inside the narrow office, across from a bookcase that I use as a catch all—purse, dog leash, books, mail, it all ends up there at some point during my day.

I take a deep breath. Quick is always best. It's my standard rule of thumb for everything. The quicker the better.

Bandage? Rip it off. Dirty cut? Douse on the alcohol. Awful, uncomfortable chats with employees? Spit it out. *Screw it.*

With one brow arched, I get comfortable and go for it. "Ready to talk?" I try asking sweetly because she looks so uncomfortable. Scared even.

Noni nods her head and breathes deeply. Her frightened brown eyes slip shut for a moment then reopen with something new in them. Courage. "I've tried for so many years to forget it," she says quietly, "but I can't. I don't think I'll ever drown those memories. Not with time, not with booze, not with men, not with drugs. Believe me, I've tried it all. It's as fresh in my mind as it was when Ed left me there bleeding." Her eyes drift from mine and her gaze settles blankly in front of her on the shelf littered with mail, receipts, and books that have yet to be catalogued. Those brown eyes lock on and Noni is somewhere else entirely.

I mentally prepare myself for what I know is coming. We just plowed right through monotony and landed square in the middle of intensity and foreboding. I know the look. She is about to recall something painful. I don't know if I should hear anything further about Damon's past, but I won't stop her. If she's mustered up the courage to talk for what is likely the first time, then I'll listen. I'll share whatever burden the memories carry with them because that's what you do. The painful parts of life are meant to be shared. They are meant to be battled by the people closest to you. Together. Sometimes we all need someone to come to the rescue. That's what Dr. Versan says, anyway. I'm still testing the theory. I guess now is as good a time as any to practice.

Noni takes a deep breath and starts to speak. "When I think about it," she starts, "I'm seventeen again and right back there." Her voice is soft but strong and her eyes are unfocused, blankly staring at that spot on the shelf.

I know that she's not here. I know that when she continues her story, she'll be reliving it. And so will I...

*"The clock on the motel nightstand reads 9:17 PM. This place is a dump. I hate it here. I can't wait until I have enough money to get a nice apartment. A real apartment of my own. It's going to be expensive but I know I could get Jackie to be my roommate. She's the first friend I made since moving here. If I share the expenses then hopefully I'll have my own place sooner than later. I told Shell that I would send her pictures when I got settled. Two months have passed since I got to Vegas and I have no photos to send. Shelly is my best friend back home in Kansas and she thought I was nuts to chase this dream. She told me that she knew I could make it here but she didn't think my very Southern Baptist family would have any part of it. She was right. My dad has all but disowned me and mom talks to me every Sunday at 9:30 after Daddy heads to bed. It's not ideal, but once I get on my feet here, I know they'll come*

*around. I'll make them proud. I'll make it as a dancer and they'll see that it's not some sin above sins to have a Vegas showgirl as a daughter. It takes talent to make it in this industry! I have high hopes for my audition. It's tomorrow at noon. That's why Ed better hurry up if he wants to spend time together tonight. I have to call my mom soon and I wouldn't dare let her know that I have a boyfriend. Well, sort of. Okay, he isn't really my boyfriend. Not yet, anyway. And what I'm doing with him is definitely something that my mom and dad would croak over. We've fooled around quite a bit but I've managed to hold him off. I know he's growing impatient though. I'm still a virgin and sex is still a little scary. Not the actual act, but the finality of it. Once my virginity is gone it's gone. That's that. I'm still preparing myself for it. Ed is older than I am and he's married, only legally though. He told me all about how he and his wife are separated and looking to get a divorce. They have a daughter together so I understand why he wants to keep our involvement private. It's tidy this way.*

*"Bev!" Ed finally knocks at my motel door.*

*I glance at the clock once more to gauge how much time I have until I have to shove him out the door for a few minutes so I can talk to Mom. Ed wouldn't intentionally rat me out, of course, but he likes a drink every now and then and he almost always gets a little rowdy after a couple.*

*"Yeah, I'm coming!" I call out. I stand and right my dress*

in the cracked full length mirror hanging on the closet door. My brown hair tumbles freely down my back, tucked back on one side with a tortoiseshell hair comb.

"Well, hurry up, girl!" Ed shouts back. It's not a good sign.

I slide the deadbolt and tentatively crack the door until the chain catches. Ed moves to push through but quickly realizes that I've not actually opened the door for him.

"What the fuck, Bev?" he growls.

My suspicions are confirmed. He's drunk.

"Open the damn door," he slurs while he teeters slightly on his feet.

"You're drunk, Ed! You know I have to call my mom in a few minutes. You can't be all loud and drunk in the background. She'll hear you!"

Ed shoves his free hand through his mussed hair and groans. "Don't be a dumb little girl. Open the damn door. You think I want anyone to know about you and me?"

The way he points his index finger at me like I'm some kind of insect makes me feel about as big as one. He does this sometimes, though, and I know he doesn't mean to hurt me. Not really. He just gets a little crazy when he's been drinking whiskey like water. I don't want to make him mad. I want him to like me and I'm looking forward to being able to tell Shelly all about my 25-year-old boyfriend when the time comes. She'll have a fit. I'm looking forward to it.

*I sigh heavily and close the door to unlatch the chain. Once it's dangling against the wood door, Ed slams it open, narrowly missing me.*

*"Hey!" I cry out. "Stop it!"*

*"Oh, stop your bitchin'!"*

*I can't believe he almost smashed the door into my face. He's being a drunk jerk already and now I'm going to have to convince him to go home. If he thinks I'm going to do anything with him tonight he is way wrong.*

*"Why don't you just go home, Ed?" I have one hand on my hip, hoping that I can be assertive enough to kick him out in time to call Mom. If I don't get in touch with her on time, she'll probably call the police and insist that they track me down.*

*Ed's face scrunches up like I've just shoved a pile of dog crap under his nose. "You want me to leave? You get me over here tonight thinking that a good time is in store and then you start in with me?" He points his finger from me to himself then back to me again and prowls three steps closer.*

*I back up until the backs of my knees hit the edge of the mattress. He's got me nervous and that is not the way to get him out of here.*

*"Look, let's just meet up tomorrow or something. I've got to call my mom in a bit and we're bickering at each other already. The night is ruined." I peer up to Ed to see if he's going to back down and I'm relieved to see that he looks both*

*very drunk and very tired. Far too tired to argue with me. Or to do other things with me.*

*"Fine. I'll just take a leak, then I'm out of here," he mumbles barely coherently as he turns towards the bathroom.*

*As soon as the door latches shut, I take a deep breath of relief and flop back onto the bed. I know I shouldn't even be seeing him. Married is married and he's too old for me anyway. Not to mention he's a blithering drunk. If it weren't for the fact that his favorite bar is directly next to this motel, I don't think we ever would've met.*

*I hear the toilet flush then the bathroom door swings open. Ed stands in the doorway glassy-eyed. The look on his face immediately spooks me and I'm on high alert. He's acting weird now and I'm scared. I've got to get him out of here.*

*"So, I'll see you later, then. I've got to call my mom." I motion towards the phone and the clock on the nightstand, which now reads 9:28.*

*Ed stands in place, unmoving except for a slight drunken teeter. He's just staring at me. His arms are hanging at his sides. My eyes drift downward to see my only washrag balled up in his hand. Great. I get one towel and one rag at a time and he's just used it. It wouldn't surprise me if he's somehow dirtied up my only clean bath towel too.*

*I sigh and decide silence is best. I'm not picking anymore* fights with him tonight. He just needs to leave and sleep off the whiskey. We can talk later.

"So..." I raise my brows and motion towards the door, hoping he'll just leave without further confrontation.

"You wanted me here tonight," Ed mumbles. "You told me to be here tonight." He finally takes a step towards me out of the doorframe of the bathroom. "You asked for it." He draws closer to me, close enough for me to see something frightening in his eyes. Cold indifference.

A voice from within screams for me to run. Adrenaline bursts through my veins instantaneously and before I know it, animal instinct has consumed me and I'm off the bed and rushing for the door.

Ed's outstretched arm catches me easily around my waist. I'm lifted and slammed onto the mattress with such force that my lungs empty. Before I can even react, his fist is drawn back, then collides with my side so hard that I think that he may have punched a hole right through my skin and bone. I've never been hit so hard in my life. I don't think. I don't breathe. I don't do anything but hurt. It's all I'm capable of. With me limp, Ed easily straddles me, his knees pinning each of my arms beneath the full weight of his body. My bones ache and feel like they could snap with even one more ounce of pressure. I begin to struggle in spite of the pain radiating through my ribs and arms. The first full breath I take is in preparation to scream. It's then that I see the balled up washrag being thrust into my open mouth.

"Please, God, help me!" I cry out from behind the cloth.

With me immobile and mostly quiet, Ed chuckles and leans back to snag my tennis shoe from my foot. I watch in horror as he pulls the laces from the eyelets where they belong. He lifts one knee from my elbow and forces my arm downward. The force of this maneuver flips me to my stomach. I have a microsecond to fight and I do. I pull and kick and flail and push, but it's all in vain because Ed has the upper hand in more ways than one. Both of my arms are behind my back and I can feel the shoelace being wrapped around my wrists then pulled tight. I cry out. I cry out so hard that it steals what little breath I have. Ed is now straddling my backside and it's clear what is about to happen. My chance to escape has come and gone. All that's left to do is survive. With his body weight holding my waist in place beneath him and the shoelace tied tight around my wrists, Ed has freedom to use his hands and he does. His clammy palm comes crashing down against the side of my head and sends a lightning bolt of pain ricocheting through my skull. My brown hair is pulled tight and my head is yanked backward so hard that I think my neck may snap. I don't feel it, though. Not with the life-saving adrenaline pumping fast through my captive body. I don't feel anything but panic and fear.

"You wanted me here," he growls into my ear. "You made me believe that you wanted it, so now you're getting it, you little prick-teasing bitch."

I can smell the pungent scent of cigarettes and whiskey on his rancid breath. I'm not sure if it's fear or the smell of him or a combination of both, but my stomach shudders in response. I gag hard again and again. I fight back against my body's reflex to puke. If I do throw up, I'll choke. I'll die. "Survive, Noni! Survive!" I chant to myself as tears pour freely down my face. I'm so scared. I want my mom and dad. I want to be home in Kansas. "Get back home, Noni," a voice from somewhere deep inside of me pleas.

So I do. I go home. If only in my head, that's what I'll do.

I squeeze my brown eyes tight and think hard about Daddy's farm as the hem of my dress is harshly shoved upward. The fields go as far as the eye can see. I miss being there. I'm dragged backward to the edge of the bed. I try harder to remember the way the fields smell when the crops of wheat and corn have just emerged from the tilled ground. Shoots of bright green wheat break through the soil and spring skyward. The scent is unlike anything else. It's the smell of hard work, perseverance, and earth all wrapped into one. It's the scent of home.

Fear grows within me still. I know what's coming but it does nothing to prepare me. My heart races in my chest and I try hard to even my breathing. With one hard jerk, my *panties are ripped from my body. A whimper escapes from behind the washrag in my mouth. I'm reminded of how scared I was the first time I drove the tractor alone. I was so nervous that I would mess something up but Dad just told me to relax and get through it. Once it's done it's done. He told me that I would never have to go through driving a tractor for the first time ever again. You only get one chance at the first time for everything. Some things you savor and some things you just have to get through. "That's life, darlin'," Dad said as he lifted me into the cab of the intimidating piece of machinery, a monster I'd seen him drive with ease a thousand times.*

*I scream loudly from behind the makeshift gag the moment I feel something hard prod against my backside. I try with all the willpower left in me to hold on to my mental retreat. I'm in Kansas. I'm not here. I'm not in this awful motel room being raped by this monster. I'm home. I'm safe. With one exacting blow to my backside, he's taken something that isn't his to take. My eyes pop open and bulge. The breath in my lungs freezes in place. I'm shocked and caught off guard by the pain. He wastes no time taking all that he wants. Another grueling stab. And another. And another until thankfully I accept the pain that has been handed to me. I stop fighting and accept it. My eyes remain unblinking. My head is turned to the side and I allow my limp, beaten, violated body to relax under his assault. With my cheek pressed to the scratchy bedspread, I cling tightly to the only lifeline I have left, my mind. My mind still fights even though my body has yielded. My mind is all I have. My mind remains untouched by him.*

*I stare numbly at the beige rotary phone on the nightstand. I should be on the phone with my mom right now, I think as it starts ringing. I hope she isn't worried. I hope she never knows what has happened to me. What has become of me? Fresh tears spill from my swollen eyes at the thought of how this would kill my family. My older brothers would want to kill Ed and I wouldn't stop them if I knew they would get away with it. My mom would be heartbroken and Dad—well, I'm not sure what he would say or do but I do know that I don't want to find out. Ever.*

*Ed's heavy breathing is louder now that his body has slowed. I hope he stops. Please stop. Please stop. Please stop. I can't stop praying to myself. I just need to get through this and shower. I need to wash it all away. I need to wash him away. I need to wash the memory of this night away. He lifts himself off of me and with one excruciating jolt of pain, he's out of me. I squeeze my eyes shut. I'm not sure why. Whether out of fear or relief, it doesn't really matter.*

*"See what happens to stupid little sluts who mess with a man like me?" he snaps at me, only an inch or two from my face.*

*A faint mist laced with tobacco and liquor lingers over*

*my skin, sending my stomach into an uproar. I gag so hard that my battered side cracks in response. A broken rib, no doubt. My eyes open wide as alarm bells resound in my head. I can't hold it down this time. I'm going to be sick with this rag shoved in my mouth. A new fear comes over me just as my stomach heaves violently. As I focus on not choking to death, I see Ed grimace in a drunken haze. He does nothing as he escapes the way he came. He left me bound, beaten, and ready for death. But I don't care. He's gone."*

I don't even know what to say. I stare blankly at her for what feels like minutes.

"I found out that I was pregnant with Damon three weeks later," she murmurs just loud enough for me to hear. I left my doctor's appointment and stopped at The Diner to spend my last few bucks on lunch. Joanne Bynum was my waitress. I remember looking at her and feeling sorry for her. She was middle-aged and working in this restaurant, on her feet all day. I remember thinking to myself that I never wanted to end up that way, working my tail off for a few bucks in some mediocre diner." She pauses and shakes her head with a bemused smirk. "When I was a dollar and twenty-seven cents short to buy lunch, Joanne gave me a knowing look and said I could eat lunch for free if I was an employee. I had nothing else, no other options, so I took the job. I never left. I became that middle-aged woman running herself ragged for next to nothing. They hired me even though I was bruised and homeless. And I was grateful for it."

# Chapter Four

## SAFE PLACE

Noni's story leaves me speechless, my face sodden with tears I didn't even know I shed. She spoke as if she was going through it all over again. As if she's still there. As if she's never left that night in a cheap motel room. Her eyes focused on that point and time in her history and she was gone from the present. I know exactly how she feels.

I'm not sure what to do at this point. I feel like sobbing. I feel like I should hug her. I feel like fighting. I feel like finding Edward and scratching his fucking eyes out for Noni and Damon.

I inhale the silence between us and scoot my chair so that we're thigh to thigh. She's sitting quietly beside me with her hands in her lap. Her eyes are still fixed to the focal point that she found at the beginning of this story. I place my hand on top of hers and just sit. It's a small gesture, but I pray it speaks volumes to her. I want her to know that I'm here. I hope she understands that this is me sharing this burden with her. This is me accepting part of the weight that she has carried for so long. This is me accepting her as she is. My sweet friend deserves so much better than what she's been given.

Noni's eyes finally drift, breaking her daze. Her tortured brown eyes lock with mine and it's evident that she's at her breaking point. Her lip quivers. Her eyes fill to the brim with more than thirty years of tears. In a flash, she sweeps her arms outward and falls, crumbles, disintegrates, her head landing on my shoulder with a thud. Tears wrack her body violently. Shoulders, arms, legs, all of her is trembling against me. My arms automatically enfold her and I do my best to gather her up against me. I'll be her leaning post if it's what she needs.

I like to think that I'm pretty tough, that I'm pretty thick-skinned, but right now, I'm not. Being in love with Damon has softened my heart more than I'd like to admit and with Noni falling apart against me, all efforts at keeping my shit together are futile.

"Oh, Noni," I croak out, pulling her tight against me like a mother holds a child, and crying with her. "I'm so sorry." The apology that I've always detested so much slips over my lips before I can stop myself. I've always hated how apologies feel. I've heard them so much throughout my life and always felt like they were never sincere—no one could ever really, truly feel regret or sadness on another's behalf. Or so I thought. Until Noni. Until right now.

I ache for her. I feel such disgust for what was done to her. I can't think of anything but how sorry I am for her, her situation, her life... everything.

"It's okay. It's okay," I repeat over and over, rubbing my hand across her shoulder blade.

After what feels like hours, but I'm sure has been mere moments, her trembling eases and her tears slow. I release my grip on her. She sniffles a few times and rights herself in her seat beside me. The dish rag that she's been carrying all day is still in her lap. She brings the soft cotton material to her tired eyes and blots away the last of her tears.

It's right then, in this very moment, that I realize that Damon is bound to find out about this at some point, and it occurs to me that my Big Man will be utterly blindsided by this information. I know he'll be surprised about Noni and frustrated with me for going behind his back (and I've been preparing myself for that backlash), but the reality of the matter, that he's here because that asshole raped a teenager... that's going to kill him. It's an alarming realization that sets my mind spinning with various scenarios on how to break the news to him, none of which are ideal.

"What about Damon?"

Noni eyes me warily as if I've just pointed a gun at her. "I-I don't know if I'm ready, Jo. I—he..." she trails off.

"We need to talk to Grams. Grams will know what to do. Grams knows everything," I ramble on.

"Jo, I'm not sure I can."

I grasp Noni by her shoulders and square myself with her. "Listen to me. Grams' is a safe place to start. We need her in our corner in case Damon finds out. *When* Damon finds out," I correct myself because there's no hiding anything from Damon. Not for long anyway. He's going to find out at some point and having Grams there for support is going to be crucial.

Noni slouches forward, cupping her head in her hands. "Beatrice is a good woman, but I'm afraid," she admits feebly.

"I am too," I confess, knowing that any attempt I make to sound tough right now would be completely transparent. Anyone in this position would be scared. I'm no different.

Nerves are a funny thing. My experience with anxiety is limited. I've never had the luxury to be scared or apprehensive until recently, really. It was always do or die for me, which left no room to be timid. Being timid was a good way to be targeted by someone with less than good intentions. Being timid would have meant being too weak to take what I needed when I needed it. I trained myself to be brazen and for the most part, it has been my favorite character trait, but right now I'd pay top dollar for some gumption to navigate this disaster. Loving people has given me anxiety, I think. I have people to disappoint now. *How am I supposed to tell him? Should I tell him? How's he going to take it? What would he do to Noni? What would he do to Edward?*

When I turn off the main road and into the driveway to our new place, my mind is still reeling with what Noni has revealed to me. No amount of preparing myself could have prepared me for *that*. Noni is fragile right now but my own sense of morbid curiosity has me wondering how she must have felt during her pregnancy with a child who was a product of her rape.

Before tears over Damon's violent conception surface again, I extinguish any thought of it. With one deep, cleansing breath, I switch off my SUV, scoop up Hemingway, and slide out of the driver's seat. Damon's truck is parked right in front, so I'm sure he's here unless he took his BMW today. A tiny part of me hopes that he isn't here. I'm not quite ready to face him knowing what I know.

Once inside, I walk straight through the house and out the back door. Grams apartment is a short trip down a walkway made from decorative pavers. Her personal quarters like a miniature version of the main house, matching exterior paint and all. I set my eyes on the small front porch and hurry to it. I need to see Grams. I ring her doorbell and shake my head, remembering how tickled she was to have a doorbell. She's a wonky old bat.

"Come on in!" I hear her chime from inside. I open her door and come to a stop when I see Grams sitting in her La-Z-Boy with a roll of utility tape, a flashlight, and her walker, her reading glasses perched on the end of her nose.

"What in the world are you doing?" I can't hide the amusement in my voice.

"I need a headlight on this thing," she answers as she peers over the top of her red reading glasses at me. "Grab some scissors, will ya?"

I hurry to her kitchen and scoop the poultry shears from the utensil caddy beside her stove. "Here." I thrust them towards her.

She juggles the roll of tape and the flashlight precariously while trying to get her wrinkled fingers into the handle of the scissors.

"Here. Let me," I insist. I lay the walker down on the carpet and kneel down on the floor to help her. "Why exactly are we putting a flashlight on your walker?" I ask as I wrench a segment of tape from the roll.

"The walkway is dark at night. I need a headlight so I can see where I'm going." It's a simple enough explanation, so I just shrug in concession. I have to admit, the woman is as practical as they come.

"That's a good idea, but I think Damon was going to have the walkway lined with outdoor lights."

"This works just as well. Why waste the money?"

"I'll let you discuss that with the Big Man," I suggest with a smile, knowing Damon will get a good laugh out of Grams' new invention.

"I will," she assures me. "Though I might patent the thing if it works out well. I can give you a cut since you did the real work."

Someone knocks lightly on the door. Speak of the devil. Damon swings it open and takes one look at the shit on the floor then at the two of us and shakes his head.

"Might I ask what you two are up to?"

"Pimpin' Grams' walker," I answer just as plainly as Grams explained to me.

"I see." He nods and holds back a smile, stuffing his big paws into the pockets of his pants. Damn, he's beautiful. It's the greatest kind of irony looking at my Big Man. He's beautiful in every way, charming and driven and generous, yet he was born out of pure evil.

I'm quick to chase away that train of thought. I eye the tape closely as I wrap it carefully around the flashlight, fastening it to the front rail of Grams' walker and tucking down all the sticky pieces. Two more strips and it's done.

"There." I smile at Grams and set her walker upright in front of her. "Now you've got a headlight."

"Beautiful!" Grams declares. "I'll call it the One-Eyed Beast."

"Please don't," I quickly respond, choking down a giggle.

Grams smiles slyly and sits back in her chair thinking up better names, no doubt. I look to Damon, who is leaning against the wall casually, looking like typical Damon. Sleeves rolled up, tie loosened, top two buttons undone exposing that delectable dip at the base of his neck, gunmetal gray slacks clinging deliciously to the hips that I so frequently have my legs wrapped around.

"It's a good idea, Grams, but the groundskeeper will be installing lighting down the sides of the walkway," Damon explains.

Grams' scoffs and looks up to my Big Man. "Well, that's just a waste. Cyclops will work just fine. No need for extra lights."

"Cyclops? That would be a great name if you two would have just gone with a headlamp versus... *this*." Damon eyes our invention speculatively.

"What? And mess up my hair? Never," Grams explains, waving off Damon's suggestion.

Laughter erupts from Damon; it's a beautiful thing. I love seeing him so carefree and happy. It's a reminder that he deserves to laugh. He deserves to be happy. He deserves so much and I plan on seeing that he gets it.

He takes a few steps my direction and pulls me to him as his laughter slows. "Thank you for helping her with everything." His whisper is feather light on my ear, causing goosebumps to pepper my skin. My eyes slip shut and I breathe in his incredible scent. Soap, and laundry, and *Damon.* "I love you, baby."

"I love you too," I whisper, feeling flush and a little dizzy on my feet.

His cell phone rings from within his pocket, breaking the enamored trance I was in. He fishes it out and screens the call. "I have to take this." He swipes the screen with his index finger and turns to walk away. "Mike, what do you have for me?" he asks into the phone as he shuts Grams' front door.

"Who's Mike?" Grams asks the same thing I've been wondering.

I shrug dismissively and get to my feet, flopping down into her new couch. This is the time to talk. I know it, but I struggle with finding the right words. "I've got a question for you, Grams."

"I've got an answer," she quips, setting Cyclops to the side.

*Spit it out,* I admonish myself inwardly. I have to get this over with. "What would you say if I told you that I found Damon's mother?" My voice is small. Much smaller than I've ever heard myself. My anxious eyes meets Grams' crystalline blue ones and all joking, jibing, and wit has abandoned her.

"What?" she whispers.

It's a rare occasion to see her so serious, but this is one of those times. I shrink marginally into the couch.

"You found her?"

A nod is the only response I can offer.

"Have you met her?" Grams' voice hasn't gone above a whisper.

"That's the... complicated part," I confess, wishing I could take it all back, wishing I could go back in time and forget seeing that birth certificate. But even if I could, it wouldn't change the fact that I've known Noni for years. We'd all be connected in some twisted way or another regardless of whether or not I learned the truth. Life can be one screwed up bitch.

"Pray tell, Jo," Grams chides sternly, tapping her foot. She's edgy now and I can't blame her. She raised Damon for the most part and he's always been hers to protect, and here I go searching out his real mom.

I inhale deeply and ready myself for the difficult story waiting to be told, but before I can say anything, Grams eases out of her seat and shuffles to her door. She cracks it open and peeks out into the backyard, looking toward the house.

"I think he's inside, but if he touches that doorknob, mum's the word. Got it? I mean it, Jo. He can't hear anything about this. He isn't ready."

I nod. She makes her way back to her recliner and settles in then looks to me expectantly. *Here goes.*

"I know her," I admit quietly, looking at my hands. "It turns out I've known her for years."

Grams watches me carefully, nodding for me to go on.

"Grams, my friend, Noni, the one I hired, is Damon's mother. I saw his birth certificate and I thought that finding her would shed some light on things, but I've known her all along. She met Damon when we first started seeing each other and recognized his name right away. I didn't know who she was until the day he proposed. Her real name is Beverly Da—"

"Child, hush!" Grams orders.

I snap my lips shut and arch my eyebrows, shocked that she would talk to me like that.

"I know who she is, Jo. I've always known. I've kept tabs on that girl since she came to my front door pregnant with Damon. Beverly Wynona Davis. I *didn't* know that you knew her, but I knew the rest. I'm old, not daft."

For the second time today I'm rendered speechless. *She fucking knew?!* "I-I thought you said you knew her first name and that was it?"

"I lied," Grams hisses. "I did a lot of that to protect Damon." A look of dismay mars her wrinkled face and I feel terrible for what I have to tell her next. She takes a deep breath before she continues. "When a little boy asks why his daddy hates him, you'd be surprised how easy it is to lie rather than tell the ugly truth." The expression on Grams' face speaks a million truths. I can only imagine how difficult it has been to be sandwiched between her grandchild and her belligerent son all these years. "Eddie hated him from the moment she handed him over to me," she says, shaking her head. "That sweet baby was the straw that broke the camel's back where his marriage was concerned, so I know part of the reason he's always resented Damon was because in his twisted way, Eddie blamed him. For the breakup, I mean. I just never understood why he resented him *so much*. It never added up for me." She clicks her tongue, still shaking her head. "It's not the child's fault that Eddie cheated on his wife and impregnated someone else. Poor Damon is as innocent as they come. Sins of the parents and all that."

"There's more, Grams." The weight of knowing is heavy. The weight of having to be the one to tell Grams what her son did to an innocent girl is unbearable.

"Of course there is." She shakes her head, obviously exasperated. "There's always more to every story, now isn't there?"

"I want you to come with me to the store tomorrow to talk to her, but not before you hear what she told me."

"Okay..." Grams says tentatively, clearly waiting for me to go on with my story.

"It wasn't her fault," I start. "Noni—S-she wasn't given a

choice. He-Edward did something unthinkable, Grams. He-he..." I can't even bring myself to say the words. I watch her realize where I'm going with this sordid tale.

Her weathered hands go to her mouth, astounded by what I've just told her. "He didn't," she mumbles from behind her hands.

"He did," I affirm.

"Oh my God." Grams shakes her head in disbelief. "Are you sure? How do you know?"

"Grams, she told me everything. She told me every horrifying detail. And the way she looked—the way she sounded—what he did to her..." I trail off, shaking my head and fighting back the lump in my throat, fighting back the tears. "It's primarily why she gave up Damon. She wasn't in a position to care for him physically or emotionally."

"Oh my God," Grams repeats, still wrought with shock. "I'll go with you to the store in the morning. I have to see her. That poor girl." Grams looks at the floor and I can see the tears pouring down her face.

I nod in understanding. I knew that Grams would want to see Noni. She's going to want to make it right. She's going to want to try to clean up after Edward like she always has.

"I told her that you were the safest person to talk to first, so please be easy with her, Grams. She's... she's fragile. And she doesn't know much about Damon's childhood. I don't know how to tell her. I don't know if I ever can."

It's the first time that I've thought about the other side of the scenario. I've been so consumed with keeping her identity a secret from Damon that I haven't even thought about what I have to keep secret from Noni. If she knew what Damon has gone through, what Edward has done to him, it would devastate her. She would feel even guiltier, like a monster instead of a victim, and Noni is not a monster. Not even close.

I stand and walk over to Grams, leaning down to kiss her on the cheek. "Goodnight, Grams. See you in the morning."

"I wish I had done more for her," Grams whispers, not looking up.

I don't quite know how to respond to that, or if I'm supposed to. "You did what you could, Grams," I say softly. "You were there for Damon."

She shakes her head, no doubt recalling what we learned from Damon's personal notebooks. "It's all in the past now, I guess," she says, patting my hand. "You're a good girl, Jo." She looks up finally and gives me a sad smile. "Night."

I leave Grams' apartment and walk up the path towards our house, wanting nothing more than to see Damon and loathing it just the same. Noni is guilty, Grams is ashamed, and I'm so damn scared of it all that I hardly know how to proceed. Plugging right through like I have been is bound to backfire soon. I have no way of knowing how this is going to play out and that's the most disconcerting for me. I'll protect my Big Man at all costs. I'll keep his heart safe even if I have to lie for a while, and it seems like Noni and Grams need to talk before anyone says anything to Damon.

Dinner is simple and relatively quiet. Damon inhales his food per usual then spends the rest of dinner watching me as close as I think he ever has. He doesn't say anything, but he never really has to. It worries me to think that he will pick up on my unease. Faking a good mood would definitely give me away. Damon knows when I'm genuinely happy and there's no faking what knowing what I know has done to my head and heart.

I ponder my situation while I do the dishes and decide to go with a simple explanation that's at least kind of true. He hasn't asked yet, because he's likely waiting for me to open up to him, but at least I'm prepared. I'll wait. If he asks what's got me in a mood, I can tell him that work was shitty today because in truth, it was.

I plod up the stairs to our bedroom, ready for him to ask what's up, and find him standing at the sink in our enormous bathroom brushing those perfect teeth of his in just a towel. One look at him and I know that he's the ideal medicine to soothe away the nightmare that was my day.

His warm eyes meet mine in the reflection of the mirror and I'm sucked into the vortex that is Damon. Every part of him summons my body to be close to his, skin to skin, eye to eye. His skin is still glistening from his shower, his hair damp and tousled, and there's just enough growth on his jaw to graze my cheek. *Flawless.*

I step up behind him at the sink and wrap my arms around him, pressing my body against his. My cheek rests against his defined back and I let my eyes slip closed for this moment of respite. Just being here with him is a welcome distraction from my chaotic reality.

"Are you going to tell me what's wrong or should I just fuck it out of you?"

I press my lips to his back, dropping little kisses as I go. "Just a long day, baby," I say mid-kiss, "but I'll take option B anyway."

Damon's body shakes as he laughs. "Don't have to tell me twice. Bed," he orders in true caveman fashion.

He turns on his heels and flicks his towel from his hips, revealing his already erect cock. It's nice seeing him naked. It's like eye therapy and I revel in the beauty of him apparently long enough for him to lean forward and haul me up on his shoulder. A girlish squeal sails out of me as I'm toted from the bathroom straight to our bed. I reach down and pinch one muscular butt cheek before he tosses me onto the mattress in a heap.

Damon crawls onto the bed, caging me in a prison made of rock hard flesh. I'm happy to serve out my sentence. I'm happy to forget all about taking Grams to see Noni tomorrow. I'm happy to forget all of it.

# *Chapter Five*

---

## FAMILY REUNION

If Grams is nervous it doesn't show. I've peeked at her a dozen times or more on the ride to the store this morning and each time she's just humming along to the song on the radio and watching the passing scenery as we zip by.

"Are you nervous?" I finally ask.

"Nah," she scoffs. "Nerves are for young people. I'm fine, honey. You?"

"Hell yes, I'm nervous. I promised Noni that this would be the easiest way to start. I don't want to be made a liar." It's a plea and a warning all in one. I trust Grams, I just don't trust this situation.

"It'll be fine, Jo. It'll all be just fine," she reassures me in that way that only a mother can.

It does the trick to settle my unrest. I nod. The rest of the ride to work is in silence.

I take a deep breath as I walk around the SUV to help Grams out. I unfold her pimped out walker and secure the locking mechanism. She smiles and steps out of the Volvo.

"After you, Grams," I say, motioning forward.

Grams oohs and ahhs over the store and I give her the world's quickest grand tour before stowing her in the office with Hemingway and some wedding magazines. I want her out of sight until I'm able to talk to Noni and let her know that Grams is here.

Noni gets to the store uncharacteristically late. I was scared that she'd skipped out on me for a minute. When I finally see her brown, lightly peppered with gray, hair, I'm pretty sure I let out a sigh of relief.

"Hey, Noni," I greet tentatively, trying to feel out her mood.

"G'morning, Jo."

*Resilient.* It's the first word that pops into my mind and I find myself admiring the woman who gave me the best gift I've ever been given. Damon. He was born out of violence and heartbreak, but he was born nevertheless. She could have gotten an abortion. She could have chosen to end his life before it had really even begun, but she didn't. She showed unwavering bravery where most would give up. I can't say that I would blame her if she had chosen a different path for herself. Faced with the same circumstance, I'm not sure I would choose to keep a child that represented something so awful.

"Are you okay?" I ask quietly.

She swallows hard and then gives me a tiny yet reassuring smile. "Yes. I think I am, actually. You're the first person to know what happened and it's the oddest thing, but I feel relieved that you know. I was thinking about it last night and decided I've been hiding it for so long that I hadn't realized how lonely my secret has made me. So," she moves forward and wraps her arms around me, "thank you."

I close my eyes and do my best to keep control over my emotions. This entire thing has reawakened feelings in me that have been dead since Maman and Papa died. I stifled them out of pure necessity. I had to be strong and being emotional simply wasn't a part of that equation. Right now, I want nothing more than to burst into tears.

Noni grips my shoulders and holds me out in front of her with an endearing smile on her face. It's enough to break down the barricade that I erected so many years ago. Stupid tears form in my eyes and I feel like a blubbering idiot.

"Ignore me. I'm being dumb," I say, swiping at my wet cheeks.

"Oh, sweetheart." Noni brings me back in for another hug that feels so good on my raw and ragged nerves that

I don't want to let go.

"I'm so emotional these days," I murmur, "it's pathetic. With the engagement, the new house, Grams moving in, the store, the wedding, you..." I shake my head and wipe a stray tear from my chin. "Speaking of Grams," I watch Noni, careful not to freak her out, "she's here. In the office."

Noni's eyes widen. Her hand goes to her chest, clutching at her heart. She stands in front of me wide-eyed but silent.

"She knows," I continue. "I talked to her last night. She wanted to see you." I pause, wondering if I should wait for a response. "Want to go see her?" I offer instead of insist.

Noni's reaction is small but it's there. She gives me a barely noticeable nod and it's go time. I walk dutifully ahead of her, opening the door to the office and revealing Grams. A small gasp comes from her when she sees Noni for the first time in over thirty years.

"My God." Grams gets to her feet and pushes the walker that I swear she doesn't really need aside. "Sweet, sweet girl," she says and opens her arms wide, welcoming Noni into them.

Without pause, Noni steps into Grams' embrace. Just like that, tears are falling from all three of us. They hug for a long time, whispering a few things to one another, none of which I'm able to hear from the doorway.

The moment finally ends when Grams pulls back and pats Noni on the cheek. I look from Grams to Noni then back to Grams. They need privacy and I need to put a stop to all this crying to get some work done. Captain would never let me live down all this girly emotion. He'd probably mutter something completely sexist about women being hormonal and therefore dangerous. He's never far from my thoughts, especially lately, and I find myself missing him more every day. Before my sentiments get the best of me yet again, I make a break for it.

"I'm going to get some work done," I offer quietly. "You two talk a while. If you need me, I'll be out here." I thumb towards the store then split.

They've got a lot of catching up to do and I have a bookstore to prepare for a grand reopening. The mountain of work waiting for me is a welcome departure from the present and I dive in headfirst.

---

I peer out of the wide, sweeping windows of our new bedroom and allow my head to swim with my beautiful, albeit complicated life scenario.

I'm lucky to have Damon. I know that better than anyone. I've never want to jeopardize what I have with him, but I fear that I've done just that. I didn't do anything to deserve his help at the scene of the accident all those years ago and I don't really feel that I've done anything special to deserve him now. Truthfully, the only thing I did was become a victim in the car accident that melded our worlds together, which wasn't exactly a choice but it bound me to him nonetheless. The outside of this relationship is a well-manicured veneer, but he and I both know that a standby therapist is a telltale sign that there's so much more that we have to work through. We look happy. We look like a couple in love and building a life together, but at the same time we're working to clear the scar tissue from our lives just to keep us that façade. It's difficult to admit, but when you compare our shitty childhoods, I think losing my parents was the better end of the deal. At least I have nothing but fond memories of them. At least I never went a day thinking that they didn't love or want me. Damon has gone his entire thirty-three years knowing that he was given up by his mother and hated by his father. I can't imagine how that reality has affected him. My heart aches more for his past than it aches for my own tragedies.

Now I've gone and taken an already chaotic situation and fueled the fire by digging into his past. I sought out the identity of his mother and now that I've got the information I wanted, I'm no longer sure that I want it. *At all.* The ominous thought of Damon discovering what I've done scares the shit out of me. Something deep down in my gut has been twisting, screaming at me to let all of this lie and pray that it settles just the way it is. A mental picture of a furious, scared, and further traumatized Damon has been tormenting me for weeks. I think the only thing that scares me more than that is the vision of a Damon that has shut down and refuses to give a shit. I waged war with that Damon once already. I won the battle, but I'm not entirely sure that I've won the war. Seeing a look of cold indifference cross his handsome face is something I never want to see again. It nearly broke me the last time. Going through it again would exhaust every ounce of my resolve.

Grams' reunion with Noni about did me in today and I'm not sure I can go any further with this. I'm not sure that I *should* go any further. I don't know how I'll be able to keep this to myself. They talked and talked and talked all day. I ate lunch with them but left them to it as soon as I had wolfed down my sub, never really entering into their conversation. Neither one of them gave it a second thought when I dismissed myself to get back to work. They kept right on talking until closing time and I ignored the nauseous feeling that my paranoia conjured up.

Damon's truck pulling into the drive draws me from the familiar murk of dismay. I watch his tall, rigid frame step easily from the cab and stride towards the front door. Just before stepping beneath the awning, his molten gaze drifts upward as if he feels me watching like I always feel him watching me. His expression is hard and I can tell he's making a beeline for me. It's difficult to tell if the tremble that's taken over me is from the thrill of anticipation that those eyes elicit or the constant, uninhibited fear of the truth coming out.

It takes all of thirty seconds for Damon to appear in the frame of our bedroom door. His wide shoulders take up all the space that the entry to our bedroom has to offer. I look to him and whether by conscious choice or reflex, I keep quiet. He stands there for a moment, looking disheveled and angry, but not speaking.

*Shit.*

My heart speeds and it has me feeling panicky. I want to say something. I should say something, but my brain is on a fucking vacation and left utter fear to housesit. Damon lifts his hand, holding up one finger, and takes long, determined strides towards our bathroom. He shuts the door behind him, leaving me confused. *What the hell?*

He opens the door a moment later looking... exquisite. He has ditched the shirt and stands in only his slacks. The way he casually props himself against the frame of the door while meticulously drying those big hands of his has me scared and licking my lips like a famished dog. God, he's beautiful. And he's mine. *Mine.*

"I—"

"Shh," he demands. He rights himself and prowls across the space between us.

The sight of him coming for me has my body thrumming with a growing need. A need for every inch of him. A need to taste him. A need to drown my worry in a sea of lust and heat. A need to be okay. The moment he easily steps into my personal space, his scent inundates me, sending me sailing over the edge in desperation.

"I want—" I begin to plea.

His hands lift to my shoulders and turn me away from him to peer back out the window. He positions himself so painfully close to my backside that I involuntarily push back against him, eager to feel him. One hand finds its way to my stomach, where he unfolds his hand wide, covering nearly the full width of my abdomen. His lips make painfully soft contact with my earlobe, sending a shiver through me in all directions like a ripple through water.

"Looks like I'm not the only one who knows how to keep secrets," he whispers into my ear. His breath against my skin is feather light, completely contradictory to the lead weight that has just taken up residence in my throat. My heart stops in my chest and fear extinguishes the fire that he so easily lit.

*He knows.*

I'm frozen in every sense of the word. The brain in my head has been taken hostage by the all-consuming fear. My feet feel as if they're cast in concrete and my stomach... well, let's just say my stomach is about to expel the sub that I so hastily ate for lunch.

Damon slips something into my hand. *Paper*. I bring it up to examine whatever it is that he has uncovered.

*A wedding magazine. A fucking wedding magazine?*

I whirl around to face him with utter incredulity written on my face. I hold it up and arch an eyebrow. "What?" I ask as coyly as I can manage.

Damon takes the magazine from me and flips casually to a dog-eared page near the middle. "Top Ten Honeymoon Destinations," he reads the title of the article that I had looked over yesterday. "You starred Paris. You never told me you wanted to go to Paris. Why not?"

*You've got to be shitting me.*

I sigh and just as if someone released the vice that my nerves were in, my body relaxes, my anxiety retreats to a manageable level, and my stomach, though still uneasy, no longer threatens to have me hugging the toilet. I shake my head at my Big Man and wrap my arms around him. "I guess I forgot to mention it to you. We don't have to go. I just... I don't know... it caught my eye since that's where I was conceived."

"Is that where you want to spend our honeymoon?" he asks pointedly.

"I don't care where we go, baby, as long as I'm your wife."

"I love the way that sounds," he admits. His hands turn greedy, exploring my backside. I moan, my forehead resting against his sternum. It's all the encouragement Damon needs.

Both hands grip the backs of my thighs just below my ass and I'm hauled up. My legs wrap around his waist as he carries me to the bed.

Damon wastes no time disrobing me. With one quick tug, he's removed the black yoga pants that I use to lounge around in. He leaves my navy blue lace thong in place but goes to work on my tank top and bra. I lie before him in just the thinnest of lace, wanton and ready. The slickness between my thighs beckons to him. His slacks drop to the floor and are joined by his boxer briefs a moment later. I squirm, watching him reveal himself to me. His engorged cock springs forward, jutting up and outward. My eyes trace every throbbing vein, every ridge and the velvety smooth rim of the tip. My tongue involuntarily darts out of my mouth, moistening my lips. Damon knows what I want.

I hold up a crooked finger and motion him to join me on the bed. "I want my lips wrapped around your cock, baby."

He climbs onto the bed and reclines on his back, his heavy cock twitching against his abdomen. I kneel between his legs, lean forward and take his length as far is it will go. The dewy tip of him butts against the back of my throat, but I take him deeper still. I peek up to see Damon staring down at me, jaw clenched, eyes heavy with pleasure.

I work my hand up and down the length of him, making long firm strokes. My tongue swirls and slides around the broad tip of his cock, winning a low moan from somewhere deep in his chest.

"Fuck, baby," he says, then sucks in air through gritted teeth. His hips begin to buck beneath my ministrations the closer I bring him to release. One big hand tangles in my brown waves, guiding me up and down.

Abruptly, his hand tightens in my hair, stilling me.

"On your back," he growls, pushing me away.

I waste no time doing just as he says and spread my legs wide for my Big Man. His fingers hook into my soaked thong. He pushes his thumb through the delicate fabric and just that quick, the junction between my legs is all his. His lips go to the soft inner part of my thigh and place warm, lingering kisses on his way to my wet center.

My hips squirm. My back arches. I ache for the fullness of him. With my eyes shut, Damon's skillful mouth reigns over the most sensitive parts of me. Purely expert flicks from his tongue overwhelm my pulsing clit. A clear moan rings out around us. It only encourages him. His full lips seal around my clit and my hips buck, my body ravenous. He alternates between light suckling and hard passes from his tongue. Little jolts of electricity burn through my extremities, making my legs twitch and jerk in sync with each pass from his tongue. My fingers find his dark chocolate brown hair, lacing through the tangled mess of strands.

"Damn you taste perfect, baby," his low voice reverberates through his lips against my flesh, setting me trembling in his grip. "So sweet."

My breathing comes in quick gasps the closer I am to coming. "Ah, Damon," I moan.

"That's right, baby," he urges.

My head tosses back against the pillow. My eyes bulge, my mouth pops open, and my body arches, giving all of me to his masterful mouth. A current of pleasure rockets through me in every direction, wiping out all cognitive thought.

He's just fucked me stupid without even fucking me. The irony doesn't escape my endorphin-saturated brain. Only my overachieving, real life God of Sex could wield this brand of magic. I'm his happy supporter.

Damon's rippled, muscular body snakes up mine, settling between my quavering thighs. My hardened nipples beg for attention and my Big Man obliges. His mouth covers my nipple briefly, sucking hard. He nips, creating the perfect amount of pain, then repeats his work on my other side.

He grips his thrumming cock and I look down to see a shining bead of dew just at the apex of his wide tip. He eases forward, placing it right on my sensitive clit, depositing his singular drop of pleasure right there. *Good fucking God, that's hot.*

My hips thrust upward involuntarily, desperately wanting to draw him in. His honey eyes burn right through me just as he thrusts into me, sheathing himself to the root. He's as deep as he can possibly go and the fullness of him is exquisite. Our respective sighs echo around us as he leans in closer, caging me. Propped on his elbows, his chiseled chest makes pass after pass against my breasts, heightening my satisfaction.

Stroke after deep stroke, Damon builds both of us closer to climax. I'm helpless beneath him. My nails dig in. My legs cling around him tightly. His breathing comes faster and heavier. His speed increases. The air in my lungs stalls in place. My toes curl painfully. My muscles clench at Damon's cock, exploiting every ounce of pleasure that he has to give. He slams into me once, twice, three, four times more, then shudders, spilling himself inside me.

With him still buried deep, I wrap my arms and legs around him, holding him close. I kiss the throbbing vein in his neck and allow both of us to relish in the bliss we bring each other.

Damon's breathing grows deep and his body relaxes against mine before I have a chance to ask him why he looked so riled up this afternoon. Whatever had him looking so tousled is a mystery. I doubt he'd do much explaining anyway. He never does. Still, I hope whatever has him frustrated has nothing to do with me. Or Noni. Or Edward.

Sleep comes easy despite my ever-growing level of worry. I only hope that when and if Damon discovers what I've unearthed, he won't pull away from everyone who loves him. Specifically me.

# Chapter Six

## SMALL ACHE

After making breakfast for myself, Damon, and Grams, I gather my things for work and shove them into my shoulder bag. I've got a laundry list of things to get done today and I pray it's enough to distract me from my own thoughts.

"Hey," I catch Damon by his necktie and pull him to me as he passes by in the foyer, "are you okay? You looked irritated when you came home yesterday."

"Versan," he explains with a shrug of his big shoulders. "Quack thinks he knows everything. That's all."

*His appointment.*

I'd forgotten that yesterday was Wednesday and that Damon would be going to see the good doctor for his usual appointment.

"Wanna talk about it?" I offer, knowing that he'll likely say no.

"Will I have to pay you?" he teases with a wink.

"Of course," I clutch my heart feigning offense.

"Name your price, ma'am."

"Hmm... Ah!" I hold up my finger then pull him closer by the silk tie he's wearing.

His lips touch mine and just like that, I'm swathed in everything Damon Cole. Even if for just a moment, I forget the world and every person in it. For just this moment it's only me and Damon and the connection we share.

"Oh, gimme a break," Grams laments in mock disgust. She's entered the foyer with her duct tape-adorned walker, a backpack slung over one shoulder, and her reading glasses dangling from her neck.

Damon's deep laugh resounds against my lips before he breaks away to smile broadly at the woman who raised him. He looks back to me and gives me a chaste peck. "Gotta go, baby. Call you later. Bye, Grams," he says on his way out of our door.

"Okay!" I call out. "Love you!"

"Love you too!" he shouts back.

Once the door closes, I look to Grams and can't help but laugh. "What's with the backpack? Going back to school?"

"No, Miss Smartypants. I've got some pictures and things for Noni to look at."

"Yeah, I guess she does have a lot to catch up on," I admit.

It's then that it really sinks in that Noni has missed almost thirty-three years of her child's life. She's given up so much. She missed watching him grow and learn and turn from a baby to a child to a man. If I ever have a child, I can't imagine missing everything. Even the thought of not seeing a baby that I made with Damon is enough to spawn a small ache in my chest. I don't like the thought. Not at all.

---

Noni beat us to work this morning and it's beginning to look like something I should expect. More often than not (with the exception of yesterday, really), I get to work and find Noni waiting to be let in. She's all kinds of dependable. Every day she even looks the same. Her brown hair is brushed smooth and pinned back with a hair comb. Her clothes are secondhand, but they're professional and always pressed and clean. She smells of lavender perfume. Her dark brown eyes are lightly rimmed with eyeliner, her lashes coated with a modest amount of mascara. I can't say that she needs much more than that. She's a beautiful woman in spite of her circumstances. Had I looked closer before, I think I might have seen my Big Man in Noni. He has the same long eyelashes, dark brown hair, and brown eyes, though his are more of a honey brown whereas Noni's remind me of melted chocolate.

I should just give her a manager's key instead of letting her wait outside with her bag lunch, purse and travel mug every morning.

"G'morning, Noni," I greet as I pull the store keys from my bag.

Grams shuffles right over to her and wraps Noni up in a hug that seems to be reserved for mothers. I'm not entirely sure how to even describe that type of hug but I do know that it's lingering and gentle and full of secret whispered exchanges in each other's ears. I take a moment to admire these two women, distractedly placing the key into the door and turning until I hear the slide of the deadbolt. I may not have my own mother around anymore, but I've gained two amazing women whom any person would be proud to call their mom. They are perfect examples of what a strong woman is. I idolize them both.

Noni smiles her typical sweet fashion. "Morning, Jo."

Grams shuffles into the store first, followed by Noni, as I prop the door open with an outstretched foot.

"I've brought the pictures I told you about," Grams says to Noni, covering her heart with her hand and smiling ruefully. "I'm excited to look at them. It's been a while."

"You two go on into the office. I've got that table guy

coming at 10," I say as I check the watch on my wrist. It isn't Maman's watch anymore and I'm still getting used to it. It's a pricey replacement though. My new Rolex matches Damon's (though I'm not sure much is the same besides the brand and the fact that it's a watch); it's a gorgeous, shiny rose gold with diamonds embellishing the face. It's simple but elegant and I must admit that I love it. I tried to refuse, but Damon insisted that I have it until he can get Maman's watch fixed after the bath water disaster. I don't know why I bothered trying to resist the elaborate gift. Damon doesn't take no for an answer. Ever. I need to remember to ask him about Maman's watch when I get home...

Grams and Noni happily retreat into the office, leaving me to begin sorting things out for the table guy. He'll be here in about an hour and since Damon is the one who arranged this meeting, there is no refusing it. He swears that this custom furniture company is the perfect thing to update the store to make it a more "young adult friendly" environment. Jonathan Greene is the guy's name and apparently he custom designs charging station bistro tables. Each one seats three customers and accommodates charging needs for e-readers, laptops, tablets, and cell phones. They even have these little pop-up partitions for privacy, making the tables look like a pie chart of some sort. His company is called Going Greene and something about it just sounds so pompous that I find myself crinkling my nose at his choice in business name.

At 9:45, the door to the store swings open an in walks Damon's assistant, Brian, a leggy blonde woman, and what I assume is her son. This must be Brian's sister. The resemblance is uncanny.

"Jo, baby, meet my big sis, Lindsay. Lindsay, Jo." He thumbs from me to her then back to me. "And this stud is my nephew, Trey."

"Stud, indeed," I say, winking at the handsome little boy. For the second time today I envision what Damon's and my babies would look like—silky brown baby hair with honey eyes and pouty, fat little baby lips. Some super feminine side of me swoons and melts into a pool of hormones somewhere on the floor. *What the hell, Jo?* I shake off the vision and focus on Brian, who's tapping his foot impatiently. "How can I help you, Bri?"

"I brought Linds with me because we're job hunting for her today, but Boss Man told me to be here to take notes during this meeting with Going Greene."

"You mean spy on me."

"Not spying! More like micromanaging in his standard way." Brian shrugs, then brushes a stray dirty blond hair from his forehead. *Must be out of hair gel.* Or spackle. Or whatever he uses to set that hair of his into a cast iron helmet-o-hair.

"You're babysitting," I toss over my shoulder as I retreat behind the coffee bar for a fresh cup. "Want something to drink, Trey?" I ask the green-eyed boy.

"Yes, ma'am," he replies politely. "Do you have chocolate milk?"

"I don't think we do, but you know, there *is* someone here who makes a wicked cup of hot chocolate. Want some?" I offer, leaning forward as if telling some national secret.

Trey's wide grin is answer enough.

"Be right back. Brian, you and Lindsay help yourself," I call as I walk off towards the office.

By the time I pry Noni from Grams and return to the coffee bar, Mr. Jonathan Greene has joined our little private party. Brian is standing there with his tablet at the ready but Trey has disappeared into the children's section. Lindsay appears to be immersed in the menu Noni has developed. Mr. Greene is standing with Brian, waiting for me.

"Hi. Jo Geroux. Nice to meet you." I hold out my hand to him.

Mr. Going Greene smiles pretentiously and I inwardly mark one for myself on the scoreboard for having predicted this. No one names their business after themselves like that unless they are truly and thoroughly in love with themselves. *Going Greene. Might as well have been Pompous Poop.*

"Pleasure to meet you, Jo. Jonathan Greene." He holds my hand for just a little too long, making this meeting awkward in a hurry.

"Yes, well, um. Let's get to it, huh?" I ask, clapping my hands together in front of me.

An hour and a half into his presentation, I find myself making up a reason to go to the office, leaving Brian to take notes from the showy Mr. Greene. I've had about all I can take of his namedropping and bragging.

When I resurface, My Greene has left the store and apparently so have Lindsay and Trey.

"Where'd your sister go?" I ask, looking around.

"I don't know, but she took off out of here like her hair was on fire. She said she'd be right back." Brian waves dismissively towards the door as if he's completely unconcerned. "I emailed you and Damon a copy of my notes. I gotta get out of here. Boss Man has already texted me twice to go get a file from Mike Passarelli," he says, shaking his head and stowing his tablet in his man purse.

"Who's Mike?"

"His personal snoop," Brian replies easily.

"What?" I make no effort at hiding the quizzical look on my face.

"Yeah, Mike just does all of Damon's personal snooping into everything business and personal. How do you not know this?" he squeaks in the most dubious fashion.

"Good question," I mutter weakly, because I really don't get why I don't already know about this guy. *Who hires someone to snoop around for them? Someone with interests to protect.*

"Yeah Mike is all macho Bruce Willis, *Die Hard* style.

He's pretty hot, too. Don't go getting me into trouble, chick."
Brian points one manicured finger at me.

"Never," I assert, holding up my hands in surrender.

"K. Later, skater," he singsongs on his way out the door.

"Peace out, girl scout," I counter.

*Snoop? Like investigator?* Guess I'll have to ask Damon
about more than just the watch tonight.

# Chapter Seven

## TRUTH TIME

When our house comes into view, I see Damon's truck parked in front. I'm surprised. He rarely beats me home.

"I'm going to have a nap, Jo," Grams says as I help her out of the car. "I'll be in later on."

"Okay, Grams. Get some rest." I follow her down the walkway to her apartment and help her in. I smile and shut the door, then hurry back into the house to get out of these clothes and see what Damon's doing. I'd like to know all about this Mike Passarelli snoop guy. I'm especially curious to learn if Mike investigated me when we first started seeing each other.

"Damon?" I call out, waiting a moment for his response. Nothing. I head in the direction of his office, betting that I'll find my Big Man in there. I tap lightly on the door then open it before Damon invites me in. I never wait for an invitation. "Hey, I called for you," I say as I enter. "What are you doing?"

Damon sits behind his desk, reading from a manila folder with a vacant expression on his face. Every nerve in my body goes on high alert. Something isn't right. He stands without saying a word and rounds his desk, striding towards the door.

Damon shuts his office door and stands himself between me and my exit. "What did you do?" he asks levelly.

My heart instantly doubles its pace and I know what's coming. I can see it in his eyes. He knows. This is happening and I'm not ready for any of it.

"What did you do?" he repeats in an eerily calm voice. The only response I can register is a series of confused shakes of my head. "Don't you deny it, Josephine; I saw you with Grams talking to her at the store."

"What?"

"CCTV, Josephine. It was installed yesterday evening."

"You were using it to spy on me?"

"That's irrelevant."

"No, I think it's completely relevant. What else have you been spying on, huh? Has Mike fed you anything juicy?" I march to his desk and snatch the manila folder up and flip it open. My eyes scan the first few lines before Damon crosses the room and seizes it from my hands, flinging it back onto the desk.

**Subject:** *Edward Cole*

**Findings:** *Substantial debt to various private lending institutions and their affiliates. No known aliases. No known foreign accounts or property. Record of two cellular numbers registered to "Edward Cole." Surveillance to continue as previously discussed.*

**Subject:** *Philippe Geroux, Collette Geroux, Josephine Geroux*

**Findings:** *Phillipe Geroux-deceased. Collette Geroux-deceased. Known relatives- Josephine Geroux,*

"Give me that!" I cry. "It's about me!"

"No. When did you find out?" Damon grates out, his jaw clenched.

Things are spinning out of control too fast. My head swims with words but all of them seem like the wrong ones.

"When?" he demands.

"I saw your birth certificate when I found the notebooks and I started looking for her," I confess feebly. "I sent the person on the document a letter. I didn't know it was her."

Damon closes his eyes tightly and drops his head. He pushes his hands through his already disheveled locks. "And?"

"She called me the day you proposed and admitted that she's your mom."

"Josephine..."

It's unclear if the way he's said my name is a plea or a reprimand. I take one step closer to him and stretch my hand out to him. I just want to make this better. I don't want him to hurt. I don't want him to know, but it's coming. I can feel his next question before he has even spoken it.

"What do you know?" His tormented gaze meets mine, leaving me unsure and frightened.

With one deep breath, I shore up what little courage I have left and prepare to confess the horrid truth. I prepare to break his already delicate heart and shatter his mind.

"Everything."

The word that carries so much comes out as a mumble. It's weighted with rape, tragedy, abuse, and lies perpetrated against Damon by everyone around him, including me. It doesn't get much worse than this.

"Elaborate, Josephine."

I hate when he uses my full name in that tone. It's a sure sign that he's beyond serious. I have nothing left to do but tell him everything and pray that he doesn't crumble beneath the burden of knowing. "Ignorance is bliss" couldn't ring truer right now.

"Damon, baby—"

"Don't! Don't you dare try to sugarcoat this right now! Tell me what you know!" He points his finger at me and bellows so loud that my ears ring in protest.

Tears sting my eyes and the knot in my throat is enough to choke on. I'm backed into a corner by my tormented Big Man with no place to go.

"He raped her, Damon," I whisper. The admission sounds so foreign. It doesn't sound like me. Maybe because I hate the truth so damn much or maybe because this is the first time I've actually said it aloud. I watch closely as Damon's brows draw up, forming a crinkled line. His attention drifts from me to the floor at my feet. I can see him mulling over my words in his head.

"Oh my God." He covers his face with his big hands and turns away from me. "Fuck!"

Damon's balled fist crashes violently into the back of his office door. The wood shudders and splinters beneath the crushing force of his fist and I startle instinctively. I've seen him angry before, but I've never seen him quite this pissed. There's far more than anger flashing in his eyes though. I see that he's hurt, devastated. I imagine not only for the misinformation he's been force-fed all these years, but also for the loss of his mother and for the unspeakable crime that his father committed. Damon knows what it feels like to be seventeen and feel as if your life has ended before it has even begun. Both he and Noni were robbed of so much by the same man. It's a link of commonality between the both of them that I hope will help them connect despite their grim history.

"Go away, Jo," he whispers, not looking at me. "I'll give

you all the money you need. Go to the penthouse for now. I'll make sure arrangements are made for you, but you have to leave here." He moves his head from side to side in little shakes, his lips pursed tightly together.

This is bad.

He strides right past me and grabs his suit coat from the chair in front of his desk, slipping into it with practiced ease.

"What? Why? I'm not going any fucking place!" I snap, all sadness evaporating into thin air. I'm partly puzzled and partly irritated. No. Scratch that. My level of frustration has just rocketed to somewhere between fuming mad and livid indignation. I'm supposed to marry this man and he expects me to tuck tail and head for the hills? He should know me better than that.

"You can't be a part of this, Jo. I won't put you at risk and I won't be able to keep my eyes on you at all times." He moves past me and rounds his desk.

"A part of what, exactly?" I demand an answer from him. He can't do something brash or dangerous or illegal, for that matter. I won't let him jeopardize himself in any way.

"It doesn't matter. You just can't be here."

"Bullshit!" My hands are on my hips and I can feel heat warming my cheeks.

"Haven't you had enough? Haven't you seen enough to know that running as far and as fast as you can is the smartest thing to do at this point?" Damon shouts from behind his desk. He has one hand planted palm down on the wood, anchoring him in place. His free hand is raised, motioning towards his destroyed office door. "I've wanted nothing but the best for you. I've never tried so damn hard to be anything for anyone. But you..." He lifts his hand from his desk and points directly at me. "Dammit, Jo. For you, I'd do anything, *except* put you at risk to be hurt. And that's exactly what will happen if you stay here." The last part of his speech makes him sound like a conquered man confessing a truth and it makes my heart sink. "I'm a constant reminder of everything negative, Jo." Damon drops into his leather office chair in a heap.

It rips me apart to see my Big Man so plagued by a past that he's unwilling to deal with. He doesn't have to accept his past—maybe not now and maybe not ever, but I do need him to accept me. If nothing else, he has to accept me, my help, my shoulder, my ear, and my love... all that I have to offer.

"You're a constant reminder, all right." I round his desk and rest my hand on his coarsely whiskered jaw. "You remind me every day exactly why I said yes. The way you look at me," I slide between him and the desk, placing myself between his legs, "the way you keep me safe," I lean forward to place a sweet kiss on his forehead, "the way you think of me first."

Damon turns his head to the side and allows me to pull him close to my chest. His arms reflexively wrap around my waist and it's a good sign that I may be winning this battle.

"The way you rescue me from myself," I continue softly, planting another kiss in the same place, "the way you look at me," I cup his cheeks, pulling him back just enough to give me the right angle to drop yet another kiss on the bridge of his nose, "the way you touch me."

His eyes slip closed as I tilt his head back and lean in to press my lips to his chiseled jaw. He sighs and I know he's coming back to me.

"The way you love me," I say just above a whisper. My thumbs stroke over his defined cheekbones until his eyes open, burning bright with pure love and lust. It's the definitive signal that I was hoping for. I've persuaded him. I've won the battle. *This time.*

His nostrils flare as he inhales deeply and his jaw clenches. A growl emanating from deep down surfaces just as his big hands take my hips into a vice-like grip, lifting me from my feet. "Loving you is all I've ever wanted to do, Jo."

My heart leaps in my chest hearing his sweet confession. Damon's expert hands glide the sash of my robe from its loops. The silk slips easily from my shoulders, revealing me to him. His eyes roam freely over my body. Nothing has changed. From the first time he took me and every time since, he takes a moment to appreciate every curve, unabashedly looking his fill.

He places one tender kiss between the swell of my breasts. He looks so defeated right now and I'd give anything to make it better. I lift my hand to tame the strands of hair that have gone astray, but he catches my wrist in midair.

He stands abruptly and covers my mouth with his in a passionate kiss that steals my breath. My tongue slides against his, battling for territory, but it's impossible to keep up with Damon. It always has been. Just as quickly as the kiss began, it ends. He breaks away from me and I see that his eyes have gone icy, stilling the heart in my chest. *No.*

"Go," he orders with such finality that I wince.

"Wh—"

"Leave."

There isn't a shred of tenderness left in him and I feel my naked body shrinking before him. For the first time, I feel vulnerable and exposed to him. I scramble to pull my discarded robe back on.

"I don't know what—"

"It's simple, Josephine. Get your things and go. I'll make arrangements for you. You'll have what you need. Brian will call you tomorrow to sort out the details."

I'm completely caught off guard. I was about to make love to my fiancé and now I'm being shoved away, tossed out—fucking abandoned! I'm sure that the confusion I feel is written all over my face. "Are you..." I begin hesitantly, scared to say the words.

"Breaking it off? Yes."

Just like that, cold, indifferent Zombie Damon is back

and I hate him for it. I shake my head fervently.

"No. You can't do this to me," I plead. "I'm sorry. Please don't do this to us." Tears break through and spill onto my cheeks.

"I just did." He pushes away from me and strides coolly from his office, leaving me. Maybe forever.

# Chapter Eight

## I'LL TRY

I didn't say goodbye to Grams and when I went to find Damon, he was gone. I slipped the diamond ring off my finger and left it sitting on Damon's side of the bed. I packed a few of my things in a daze and drove myself back to the penthouse in silence. I couldn't cry. I couldn't think. All I could do was replay his words in my head. Damon left the house before I did and is likely forgetting me over a bottle of booze right now. Maybe even a woman or two.

Thoughts of Creamsicle Carrie, that slut of an interior decorator, and various other plastic women falling over themselves to get ahold of the newly single Damon Cole bombards my shattered heart with mental images I'm far too fragile to entertain at the moment. I wish I had the stomach to drink. I could go for a glass of wine or two. Or ten. Instead, I rummage through the fridge in the kitchen and manage to dig out a freezer burned pint of chocolate chip cookie dough ice cream to drown my sorrows in.

"Jo? Baby?" Brian calls.

"I'm in here," I say around a mouthful of cookie dough.

Brian steps into the bathroom reeking of condolences and sympathy. *Fan-fucking-tastic.* "Oh, honey," he coos with his bottom lip rolled out mocking a look of dismay.

"Don't. I can't—I... *Fuck!*" It's next to impossible to keep the emotion out of my voice. Rather than face him, I slip down under the bubbles of the full tub I'm soaking in and let the water wet my hair completely. I resurface to see Brian sitting on the toilet across from me.

"Why are you in here?" he asks, looking around at the guest bathroom.

"Because it doesn't make me want to die." My answer is simple and couldn't be more true. The master suite here at the penthouse is full of memories that I can't bear to revisit right now, especially with the prospect that those memories may be all I have left of Damon.

"Oh," he says knowingly, focusing on his neatly folded hands.

I flip the toggle on the spigot back and forth with my toes, staring straight ahead.

"Come on. You can't sit in there forever." Brian pulls me

to standing and hands me two folded towels. "There's a robe right over there, sweetie. I'll wait for you in the living room."

After drying off and wrapping myself up in the robe that Brian left me, I venture out into the living room to find him on the phone with his back to me.

"She's a mess, Boss, but I'll stay with her tonight. Okay. I will. See you in the morning." Brian hangs up with Damon and turns to see me openly eavesdropping.

Just knowing that the man that I am irrevocably in love with was just on the phone makes the ache in my chest grow exponentially. I'm cross-eyed jealous. I want to hear his voice. I want to know what he's doing. Where he's at. Who he's with. What he's thinking. I just want him.

"Sorry, babe. He made me promise to check in once I talked to you."

"Does he even give a shit?"

"Of course he does, Jo. The whole reason he pushed you away is because, in his messed up way, he cares. He thinks he's protecting you," Brian explains with a shrug, patting the couch next to him. "I think this will blow over. Just give him time. I don't know the whole story, but what I do know is that Damon loves you, probably more than you even know."

I scoff at his sentiments. I can't convince myself that he loves me even a fraction of how much I love *him*. If he did, he wouldn't have sent me packing so readily. I said I was sorry. I was just doing what I thought would help. I want Damon to stop living in the past and move towards the future I thought we wanted together. I couldn't help but think that finding his biological mom would somehow help him find closure. Now I know that I was wrong and apparently didn't know the man I love well enough to make that sort of judgment call.

"I can't hold onto hope," I reply sadly. "It hurts to think that I could hope for him to calm down just to be let down when he never calls."

"I know." Brian sighs. "Men, huh? Come on, let's watch a movie or something."

"I don't really feel like it, Bri. I think I'm just going to go to bed."

"Are you sure?"

"Yeah, I just need to sleep. I'm so tired."

"Okay... Want me to stay?"

"No, you go on home. I'm sure I'll see you tomorrow."

"Pshh! You can count on it," he says complete with dramatic flair and I can't help but smile weakly at this man who has become my closest friend. "Call if you need me and I'll be right over," he promises as he picks up his man purse and heads for the door.

"Okay. Night," I mutter. I refuse to keep him here to watch me bathe in misery, nor will I be one of those women that force their best friends to endure hours of lamenting over a breakup.

"Night, doll."

For no reason other than my aptitude for self-destructive behavior, I find myself in the library, Damon's domain. The penthouse was left furnished since Damon bought new furnishings and décor for the new house. The shelves in the library are still full of the best literature to be had; the couches and chairs that Damon took me on so many times are in the same places they always have been. I walk to the arm of the oversized chair that holds countless memories of Damon claiming my body and let my fingers drift lightly over the fabric, remembering how it felt against my bare body, recalling Damon filling me. I sit down in the chair and press my thighs together. I squeeze them tight, trying to mollify the growing need at my center. I ache to feel him against me. I ache to feel him in me. I ache to feel him beside me.

A bone-quaking sob rips through me as reality sets in. I've just lost my Big Man. I've just lost Damon to a past that refuses to go away. He's stuck there and I'm stuck *here,* feeling helpless to save him from the darkness that looms over him and, subsequently, us. It's not something that I can kiss and make better, but I'd try if I could. I'd try if he allowed me the chance.

Damon grips my chin between his index finger and thumb, then strokes the pad of his thumb achingly slowly over my bottom lip. My eyes slip shut, relishing in the desire that he builds within me. Something deep in my core cries out for him. Damon must hear my unspoken pleas, because his fingers curl around the nape of my neck, pulling me in to claim my mouth with his. His warm, wet tongue slips over my open lips and dives deep into my mouth, caressing my tongue as it slides against his tantalizingly slowly. His hips roll against mine, winning a moan from me. I want him. I've never wanted someone so badly. I've never needed someone so badly. The kiss ends when Damon breaks away, leaning his forehead against mine. We're both panting and eager. The rigid bulge in his slacks presses against my abdomen, teasing me. My fingers slip through the belt loops of his pants and I pull him closer to me.

"I love you," he confesses as if it pains him. As if he loves me so much that it hurts.

I know how he feels.

"I love you too," I whisper, my lips grazing the dusting of hair on his chest. "I love you so damn much."

Damon takes a deep breath then takes my mouth all over again. He smells so good. I can smell his body wash and his cologne and his freshly laundered clothes. Tears build in my eyes and I'm not sure why. I know he's here with me. I can see him and feel him and taste him, but something inside feels so broken. Something inside of me feels like this is the last time and I think I could lie down and die.

"Don't leave me," I beg, breaking away from his kiss.

Damon says nothing. His luminescent eyes just peer into me.

"Damon?" I ask, stepping away from him. He does nothing still. "Damon!" I cry out, wanting to hear him say that he'll never leave me alone.

I'm startled awake to find myself still in my robe in the chair in the library. Tears have seeped from my eyes. I look around the dimly lit library, trying to get my bearings. My dream was so vivid, so real. I could feel his skin. I could feel the warmth of him pressed against me. I could smell him just as if he was in the room with me. Realization hits me like a freight train. I jump up and run downstairs. I come skidding to a stop at the kitchen island when I see a note.

*I'm sorry. I never wanted to hurt you. I hope you'll forgive me one day.*
*—D*

My eyes scan the note three times in a row. *He was here.* He was here. I could smell him. I can *still* smell him. I clutch the note to my chest and sink to the floor against the kitchen island.

It's really over.

I've never been so heartbroken.

# Chapter Nine

## BURNING BUILDING

It's amazing at the things that can happen in a matter of two weeks' time. I've eaten a bunch of junk. I've slept. A lot. I've watched one chick flick after another even though they make me feel worse. Yet another example of my propensity for self-loathing.

I haven't seen much of Grams. I've spoken to her twice, both times cut short by my lacking intestinal fortitude. I made an excuse to hurry off the phone because talking to her just hurt too much.

Hemingway is the only one who doesn't mind my wallowing. Brian dropped him off that next morning after Damon kicked me out. Hemingway is just happy that I'm almost always home. I pop into work for the things that I *have* to be there for, but otherwise I avoid the store. It hurts even being there. It hurts knowing that it was the very place where I met Damon for the second time. Walking into that place is the equivalent of walking into a burning building. I hold my breath and run in, do what I have to, and make my escape before the flames consume me.

Noni doesn't seem to mind. She hasn't said much about anything except for the occasional "I'm here if you need to talk." Other than that, she's been doing a fine job of working her tail off to get things ready for the grand reopening that I'd prefer not to attend. She deserves a raise. I figured the least I could do was give her the keys to Captain's house. She insisted on paying rent, but I told her that she was free to stay there as long as she paid the taxes and managed the expenses for maintenance and upkeep. She agreed and ditched her old apartment in the dodgy part of town the next day with a promise that she'd find a way to buy the property off of me one day. I told her that she was doing me a favor by moving in, but she still thinks that I was being too generous. She's crazy.

The extent of my social life has consisted of fast food with Brian and chatting with Howard, the security guy, on my way out to walk Hemingway. I've bumped into Handy Andy almost every day when we're out on a walk and I'm starting to see that it's no accident. He's been kind and understanding that I'm a heartbroken train wreck right now, and his flirtation has been kept to a minimum. Thank God. He walks his black lab, who I named Chaucer. We meet in about the same place every evening and sometimes we let Hemingway and Chaucer off their leashes for a run in the dog park. It's been a nice distraction.

I haven't heard from Damon since the note he left on the kitchen counter fourteen days ago. He sends messages via Brian and that's it. No phone calls. No texts. No emails. Nothing.

He gave me the store, the Volvo, Hemingway, and use of the penthouse for as long as I want. I told Brian to go cram Damon's settlement agreement up his ass. I don't want his fucking money. I want him. I want our lives together. He's taken that, the most valuable thing to me, so throwing money at my wounded heart doesn't do anything but insult me. Brian says that Damon is only trying to help, but I'm not in any kind of mood to entertain his magnanimous efforts.

Hemingway groans beside me on the couch, getting my attention. I set my book down and look down to the little monster.

"What's up, Hemingway? Need to go potty?" His loud *yip* is a resounding "yes" in Schnauzerranian. I would know. I speak Schnauzerranian fluently now thanks to an intensive two week long immersion course courtesy of my breakup with Damon.

I kick off my pajama shorts and slip into a pair of denim

capris that fit a little more snugly thanks to my recent binge on everything processed and high in fat content. I can't help but roll my eyes at my own petulance. I slip on my flip flops even though it's a little chilly with the sun low in the sky and scoop up Hemingway for the trip downstairs. I'm thankful for Vegas weather. My wardrobe is pretty much the same year round. As long as the sun is up I can get away with sandals nearly every month except January.

"Hey, Howard," I greet as I walk passed the security desk.

"Evening, Miss Josephine."

"Are you ever going to call me Jo?"

"Probably not," he says, and the stony-faced bastard actually cracks a smile.

I'm as shocked as a person could possibly be and I can't help but smile back since it's such an occasion. "How is your evening?"

"It's okay, I guess." Howard's moment of lightheartedness quickly fades. His eyes drift and though it may be unwelcome, I offer an ear.

"Something wrong?"

"It's nothing, Miss Josephine."

"Are you sure? I don't mind talking for a bit." I step closer to the security desk and lean against the counter.

"It's just some bad news I got today. My dad has Parkinson's and the medication isn't helping much anymore. He can be put on a new group of medications but it's just too expensive for me and my brother."

"Howard, I'm so sorry to hear that. If you're anything like your father, I'm sure he's a sweet man who doesn't deserve this."

Howard nods and gives a polite smile signaling that he's done talking about the subject. I imagine he feels terrible that he can't help his father. If I were in the position to do it, I'd give him the money he needs.

"Well, I hope things work out for the better. Let me know if there's something you need. I'll be back later, Howard," I offer as I back away from the counter and step out into the cool evening breeze.

I set Hemingway onto his furry feet and start out on our normal route, stopping at all his favorite patches of struggling desert grass. Andy and Chaucer come into view just as I've come to expect. We walk toward each other, our respective dogs leading the way. Hemingway dances around, excited to see his walking partner.

"Hey, Jo," Andy says, his smile showing off his dazzling teeth and dimples.

"Hey to you too, snazzy dresser!" I give him a once over, marveling at how nice a suit looks on his hefty frame. "What the heck are you doing walking your dog in a suit?"

"Ah, well I was hoping a walk could butter you up first but, since you asked... I have this dinner reservation. My date bailed on me so I was kinda hoping..." His blue eyes survey me cautiously.

"Oh, um, I don't know, Andy," I reply quickly. "I'm not dressed and I'm not in the mood for real food. I—"

"Come on, it's just friends taking advantage of good food at a nice place that has the waiting list from hell. Come on. Please?" He steeples his hands in front of him and mocks begging, even puffing out his lower lip.

I tilt my head to the side, contemplating how much effort it would take for me to get presentable and pretend I'm not doing battle with a shattered heart. "Oh what the hell," I resign, tossing one hand outward. How bad could it be? I've got to start living again at some point. No time like the present. "Just friendly, *platonic,* dinner," I say sternly and Andy nods his head as I speak.

"You got it." He beams another Handy Andy panty-dissolving smile and I roll my eyes at him. "I'll come get you at 7. Dinner is at 7:30."

"Sounds good. Just have Howard, the security guy, buzz me and I'll meet you downstairs in the lobby."

"Okay, see you at seven, Jo."

"See you then."

---

I showered and dried my wavy brown locks in record time. I didn't bother shaving my legs, given the obvious. Picking out something to wear hasn't been as simple. Two outfits looked entire too sexy to be worn on a dinner date with a friend. Another outfit was too damn tight but this one is perfect.

I examine my reflection in the full length mirror and give myself a thumbs up. The gray sheath dress looks great. It isn't too sexy or too tight and it isn't pajamas—a win in my book. Coupled with nude patent leather peep toe pumps that *aren't* Jimmy Choo, the dress looks ideal.

I hurry and line my eyes, coat my lashes with mascara, dust on some eye shadow and blush, spray on some perfume, and I'm out the door. I toss my waves over my shoulder in the elevator on the ride down to the lobby, feeling the tiniest bit human again.

The elevator chimes, coming to a halt, and the doors slide open. I step out to see Andy chatting up Howard at the security desk. Howard eyes me like I'm public enemy number one. I ignore his obvious disapproval. He's clearly being loyal to Damon, but that's just uncalled for. I'm not the one who ended our relationship, and besides, I'm going to dinner with a *friend*. He's no different from Brian. Well, minus the whole gay thing and the striking difference in physical appearance, I guess.

"There she is. Nice to meet you, man," Andy extends his hand to shake Howard's and we leave the lobby. Andy motions for me to take his crooked elbow.

I look at him hesitantly. "Um, should we take my car or yours?" The discomfort rings loud and clear in my voice.

"Neither. The restaurant is just down that way." He points down the block.

"Oh. Okay."

"Come on." He urges me to take his arm and I just stand here like an idiot, unsure of how to act. My experience with platonic dates with extremely attractive *straight* men is... nil. "It's nothing, Jo. Promise."

I sigh deeply and slip my arm through his for the walk.

Ga Tan is the name of the place. The restaurant is nice. Really nice. I've seen the place but I've never been inside. It's upscale French-Vietnamese fusion with fresh floral centerpieces, pressed linen, crystal glasses, and waiters that know their stuff.

We're seated immediately and scan over the limited menu that doesn't even have prices on it. That's when you know you're in a pricey joint. No prices=expensive.

"What do you want to drink?" Andy asks, looking up at me from his menu.

"Um, I'll stick with water for now." I really would love a drink, but I probably shouldn't. An alcohol-soaked brain is the last thing I need. That would have one night stand stamped all over it.

A bow-tied, gilded waiter appears and Andy is quick to

wave him over. "I'll have a scotch on the rocks and my date would like water, thank you."

The waiter nods and scurries away to retrieve our drinks.

"She must've been some catch if you made a reservation at this place," I say, leaning forward, whispering discretely in the intimate atmosphere.

Andy smiles tightly and shakes his head.

"What?" I ask, my voice no longer so quiet.

"I made this reservation for you." He cringes, obviously waiting for my reaction.

He's right to cringe, because my first instinct is to leave his ass here, but how could I possibly be mad at the guy? It's no secret that he has thing for me. He's made it clear since we met at the old folks' home that he's interested and he flirts incessantly, so it's not like I'm entirely surprised that he would go so far as to trick me into a date with him.

I just stare at him while I toss around this information in my muddled head.

"Please don't be mad. Can you blame me for wanting a shot with you?" he asks, looking downright pathetic. Not pathetic in a bad way, more like pathetic in a sad puppy kind of way.

"I'm not mad, Andy," I admit. "I'm just—I don't know what I am," I grumble.

"Look, no pressure. We'll just have dinner and leave it at that. I'm not trying to rush you, Jo."

"Okay."

It's the only thing I can say right now. What am I supposed to say? *Andy, while I'm flattered that you'd go so far as to trick me into having dinner with you, and you're definitely fuckworthy, you'll never be enough because I'm still hopelessly in love with a man who doesn't want me.* That response is most definitely not on my list of things to say. Ever.

Ordering food is a game of Russian roulette that I happen to do well at. I don't know what the hell I'm ordering because the menu was in some sort of strange French-Vietnamese melded language (neither of which I speak nor read), so I picked at random. Turns out, I chose divinely, and being that it's the first real food that I've had in two weeks, I savor every morsel.

"Gosh, that was good." I sit up straight as a board in an attempt to ease my full belly.

Andy's gaze drops to my breasts. His eyes drift back to mine and something unspoken lingers in the air. He wants more. He wants all of me. Any other red-blooded American female would take him up on his nonverbal offer. He's tall and handsome. He's rippled with muscles. He's got a gorgeous smile and beautiful blue eyes. He has a job. He has a job. He even has a Labrador retriever, for God's sake!

I wait a moment to see if the purely female part of me is inclined to reciprocate his silent offer, but nothing.

Apparently, even the purely female part of me is still hung up on Damon.

"I'm going to go to the bathroom," I say, suddenly anxious. "Be right back." I slip from the table before he can even respond. I can feel him watching me as I nearly run to the ladies' room.

I shut the bathroom stall door and latch it. I don't really have to pee but I absolutely need a breather. With my palm pressed to the back of the door, I close my eyes and work at calming my nerves. This is bullshit. I can't act like this every time a man who *isn't* Damon Cole makes a pass at me. If this is what's in store for me for the rest of my life, then I vow to never date again. This is misery personified and I'm about full up on that particular emotion.

After a brief reprieve, I smooth my dress and slide the lock on the stall door. I step out of my current nightmare and right into another.

Creamsicle Carrie is standing at the bathroom vanity smearing on a terrible shade of pink lipstick.

I step up to the sink and begin washing my hands. Creamsicle catches my glare in the mirror and about falls over. It's a nice reaction that has me inwardly adjusting the scoreboard again.

"Carrie," I greet curtly.

She does a decent job rebounding because she turns to face me with a limited smirk on her Botoxed face. "Heard about your bad news," she says, feigning sympathy.

"I'm sure you did. Everyone knows." I shrug, pretending that I'm not dying of a broken heart.

"Yeah, Damon told me all about it," she adds and it feels like a blow to the gut.

*Bitch!* I reach for the plush hand towels that are so nicely stacked for patrons and a visual enters my head that includes me wrapping this hand towel around her scrawny neck and twisting it like a bread tie until her stupid head pops off like one of those robot toys. It's an appropriate comparison when you think of the plastic and/or artificial ingredients ratio. She has about the same amount of organic material left in her as the robot. Both completely manufactured. Fake boobs, fake tan, fake hair, fake nails, fake jewelry, fake designer clothes, fake teeth—her name is probably fake too!

The mental picture is a great method of distraction, because a slow smile eases across my face, exposing my own pearly whites. "Nice to see you, Carrie. Let's do it again on the tenth of never," I reply, tossing the towel her direction and walking right past her.

Her face contorts in an attempted show of displeasure and I take a second to enjoy it.

# Chapter Ten

## PEACHY

I'm making my way back to my table when I feel eyes on me; it can't be Andy because he isn't even in view yet. I stop in my tracks when I realize that the only other person who has ever made me *feel* their gaze is a certain tall, dark, and handsome man with a predisposition for breaking hearts.

I turn in place and lock eyes with him in all his screwed up glory. Instantly, a lump forms in my throat and even though my brain is screaming for me to run, I can't. I'm maybe four feet from his table and caught up in his molten honey gaze.

"Hi," is the only thing that comes out.

"Josephine," he says just as curtly as ever. There isn't a trace of emotion in his eyes and it's like a knife to my heart.

I break our staring contest, looking over to the man he's sitting with. "Hi, I'm Jo." *And I'm stuck on stupid.*

The bald man extends his hand to me and I take it. "Mike," he says warmly. "Nice to meet you."

Brian's description of Mike Passarelli comes to mind and I make the connection. *Bruce Willis. Die Hard.* I must admit that Brian nailed that one. The description, not the man. This is Damon's personal snoop, as Brian referred to him. I look down at their table and see something that taps the nail into the coffin.

There it is, like a big, fat middle finger. A wine glass with a lipstick stain in the shade of hideous. *Carrie.*

I could kill him right on the spot. I could strangle him with my bare hands. How dare he? Carrie? Of all the bimbos traipsing around this town, he has to pick her to rebound with? My eyes linger on the stupid glass for a moment as I fume. I look back up at Damon and do my best to look unaffected but it's no use. My inner heathen has won this one. Game, set, match. I lean forward, coming dangerously close to him. My lips are a hairsbreadth from his ear and I let loose.

"Fuck. You," I whisper as if it was an offer rather than an insult, but Damon knows better. The syllables are fortified with pure venom concentrated by weeks of lonely nights and bleak days. I hope that it cuts him deep, but it likely won't. I right myself, turn on my heels, and march right back to Andy with Damon's penetrating stare burning holes through my back until I'm out of sight.

"Let's go," I demand like a criminal making a run for it.

"What?" Andy's blue eyes are confused. Poor guy.

"I want to get out of here. Now." I snag my purse from the back of my chair and sling it over my shoulder. He had better move or I'll leave him here. I can't stay in this place. Just breathing the same air as Damon right now is upsetting.

"Uh—all right. Is everything okay?" he asks nervously, tossing money on the table.

"Yep. Peachy. Damon is here." I walk ahead of him out of Ga Tan and into the night air. I inhale deeply through my nose, allowing it to fill my lungs from top to bottom.

Andy stands beside me, watching dutifully and giving me a moment to shake off my unpleasant exchange with Carrie and Damon. Just thinking of her grubby fingers all over Damon makes me want to hurl and break something and claw out her eyes and kick him in the nuts then inhale a spread of comfort food like it's a medicated balm to soothe my wounds.

We walk arm in arm back to the penthouse in silence. He doesn't asked for details and I haven't offered them.

Andy tugs my arm, bringing me to a stop on the sidewalk just before the penthouse. "Hey, what's wrong?" he probes.

My head drops. My answer is simple and honest. "Damon and some orange-colored broad that has a way of crawling right under my skin."

Andy's hand goes to my chin, tilting my head up to look

at him. Tears don't threaten. I'm too tired to cry. I'm past crying and smack in the middle of general dismay.

"You are an incredibly beautiful, smart, driven woman who could have your pick of any man in this city. Don't let one man ruin the rest of them for you."

"Thank you, Andy," I breathe. He's right. I know he's right, but it's far easier said than done when said man happens to be the love of your life.

His attention drifts to my lips then back up to my eyes, asking permission. There isn't any reason why I can't or shouldn't kiss him. He's sweet and attractive and he likes me. He's been a gentleman all night. If Damon can rebound already, so can I! *Just a kiss. No sex. No relationship. Just a kiss*. I chant over and over to myself like it's my new mantra— *Just a kiss*.

Andy's mouth lands on mine; he kisses me softly, coaxingly. I return the sensual kiss, hoping that it will stir something within me. A part of me hopes that kissing another man will rid me of some of my need for Damon. Andy's fingers lace through my hair, pulling me closer, intensifying the kiss. His warm hands hold me immobile as he takes the breath from me. He takes and takes some more. He groans in appreciation then slips his tongue over the seam of my lips, gaining entrance to my mouth.

While he's a great kisser, he isn't Damon. A vision of a furious Damon bombards my thoughts and I break away from

Andy. It's so ridiculous, but I almost feel like I'm betraying Damon—like I'm cheating; like I'm giving away something that doesn't belong to me, but to him.

"I'm sorry. I just—I can't," I mutter, wiping my lips with the back of my hand.

Andy squeezes his eyes shut and sighs in apparent disappointment and I can't say I blame him. I'm disappointed too. I wish Damon didn't dominate every part of me, but he does. At least for right now.

"I'm just going to go ahead and go to bed. Thank you for dinner," I say cordially, fidgeting with my fingers in front of me, not knowing what else to do.

"Thank you for not taking off when you found out that I tricked you into coming." Andy smiles sweetly, tucking a strand of hair behind my ear. "Want me to take you up?" He motions with his chin toward the penthouse behind me.

"Nah. I'm fine. I'll see you tomorrow?"

Andy nods. "You know where to find me." He turns his broad shoulders and walks away, leaving me alone.

I stand on the sidewalk feeling homeless again, physically and emotionally destitute. My home isn't really my home, it's Damon's. And my heart isn't really my heart. That's property of Damon Cole too.

# Chapter Eleven

## BROKEN AGAIN

I walk past the abandoned security desk and take the elevator up. The moment I'm through the door I kick off my heels. One by one they skitter across the floor. I drop my purse strap on the banister of the stairs. The thin belt around my waist is next. I unbuckle it and pull it from the loops holding it in place. It drops to the stairs. Once I'm on the landing, I reach around and unzip my sheath dress, letting it slink to the floor. I've discarded everything haphazardly, needing desperately to sink into a hot bath. I can clean up my mess later, but right now soaking away my encounter with Damon takes precedence.

Water feels good on my face. I wipe away the makeup and examine my reflection in the guest bathroom mirror. I look pathetic. My eyes are tired. My shoulders slouch involuntarily. My muscles have softened with lack of use. I'm the poster girl for depression.

A loud crashing noise coming from downstairs has me standing still, listening closely for the culprit. It's impossible to break into this place; it's as secure as they come. I struggle to recall if I engaged the security alarm when I came through the door. *Fuck!*

I scurry to the closet looking for something, anything, to arm myself with before I go downstairs. Even if there was a weapon in this closet I doubt I'd be able to find it beneath the clothes, shoes, and random junk that's strung all over the place. Housework has been at the bottom of my priority list lately.

I don't even have my cell phone since it's at the bottom of the stairs in my purse. I go over my options in my head for a moment while I stand in the closet in just my bra and panties.

I know my best bet is to get my phone and call the security desk. If I call whoever is on duty tonight, they can come up and check things out for me or call the police on my behalf, whichever comes first.

I peek out from my hiding spot to make sure the coast is clear then tiptoe to the guest room door. I peer into the dark hall looking for the first sign of trouble. I don't see anything, so I tiptoe down the hall to the landing at the top of the stairs.

"Holy shit!" I nearly jump out of my skin when I see

Damon coming up the stairs with my shoes, purse, and belt in hand. "What the fuck are you doing?" I screech. "You scared the hell out of me!" Blood rushes to my head, my ears ring, and my cheeks redden thanks to the copious amount of adrenaline humming through my veins.

"Where is he?" Damon growls, looking right past me.

My eyebrows furrow. "Who?"

"Is he here, Josephine? I'll kill him," he mutters and walks past me.

"Hey! Where do you think you're going?" I scurry behind Damon.

"Andy. Where is he?" he grates out, his jaw clenched tight and a muscle ticking in his cheek. He's a walking time bomb of testosterone.

"You're joking, right?" I can't hide the disbelief in my voice. "Where's Carrie?" I snap, bursting forward to step in front of him.

"Don't toy with me, Josephine."

"I'm not toying with you. I'm dead serious. What gives you the right to barge in here, scaring the shit out of me, might I add, just to try and dictate *who I'm seeing*?" I embellish the "who I'm seeing" part for effect. I'm in no way, shape, or form *seeing* Andy. He's a friend and I don't plan on taking things beyond that.

"This is my property," Damon answers simply, eyeing my scantily clad body. The way he's declared that this is his property has me wondering if he's talking about me or the penthouse or both.

A thick vein in his neck bulges and palpitates, displaying how pissed he is. Something about an angry Damon sets my insides stirring. It always has. *Stop!* I reprimand myself. Turning on my heels, I stomp off to the guest room, desperate for space and clothing.

Damon's footsteps match mine as he walks close behind. He's goddamned impossible.

"Privacy? Have you heard of it?" I grind out over my shoulder.

"I've seen your body a thousand times, Josephine. Don't be a child."

"A child? A child? Who's the child walking around acting like the whole world belongs to him and people should just watch out, else be squished beneath your shining fucking Oxfords?!"

Damon's eyes widen, apparently shocked by my insult.

"Just leave, please." I scramble for something resembling pajamas. A robe. A towel. Even a scarf would be better than standing here in my panties and bra.

"Are you fucking him?"

I gape at his forwardness. "That's none of your business, Damon," I assert, shaking my head at how stubborn and persistent he can be. I snatch my robe from the floor, slip it on and turn to face him.

"It damn sure is my business!" he roars.

"No. It's not," I reply calmly. "That's the funny thing about ripping a person's heart out and walking away from them. It means you no longer get a say in anything that person does." I talk to him as if he's a child, pointing from me back to him.

"Jo," he breathes, shoving his big paws through his dark hair.

"He's just a friend, Damon, and he damn sure isn't here," I admit feebly. Part of me wants to let him stew in his mess, wondering if I'm seeing Andy, but the part of me that's still so completely in love with him hates to see him upset. Irrational or not, in my heart, he's still mine and I'm still his.

"Jo, I—" Damon visibly struggles with whatever he's wanting to say.

My heart leaps, hoping that maybe he's changed his mind, that maybe he's realized that anything I ever did was because I love him so much. I watch him closely as his beleaguered eyes work at what he wants to say.

*Nothing.*

And with that, my heart breaks all over again.

"You can't do this to me," I whisper with a quivering chin. "You can't make this ugly. A clean break is the only way I'll survive this. It's the only way I'll survive losing you." I make no effort at hiding the tears that have welled in my tired eyes.

Damon's eyes slide shut. He shoves his big hands into his

pockets in his customary way and turns away. Just like that I'm broken all over again. I've lost him for the second time in a matter of two weeks.

# Chapter Twelve

## THE COLOR OF SNOTTY

I stagger into the store after a night of tossing and turning. What little sleep I did get was dominated by dreams of Damon and the life we won't be sharing together. Coming to the store this morning is actually far better than lying in bed feeling depressed.

Brian comes skipping into the store (literally) about an hour after I do with an annoyingly chipper disposition that I'm sure is thanks to a night full of sexual exploits. "Good morning, doll," he singsongs, sounding all Broadway *Cats* meets *Will & Grace*.

I scoff at him, mostly out of jealousy. It's nearly infuriating seeing happy people right now. Here I am opening box after box of deliveries feeling like death and Brian is acting like he's a cast member of *Mary Poppins*. "What's so damn *good* about this morning?" I bemoan.

Brian halts in his tracks as if someone has clotheslined him. "Eww. Snotty really isn't your color, Jo. PMS much?"

I feel guilty almost instantly. He doesn't deserve my shitty attitude. "I'm sorry, Bri. I'm just tired," I lie.

"Awe, it's okay. I forgive you," he smiles and winks.

"What are you doing here?"

"Okay, so don't shoot the messenger, but Damon sent me here."

"What for?"

Brian motions towards the office and I lead the way. Once in the office, he squats to pet Hemingway, who is lounging under my desk as usual. Brian ruffles the hair on Hemingway's head then holds his hand out to me. "Got any germ stuff?"

"He's a dog, Brian. Not a corpse."

"Same difference. Both are germy." He shivers in mock disgust.

"Has anyone ever told you how ridiculous you are?"

"Of course," he replies with a bright smile in place. He's proud and confident in his own skin. I envy him. "Anywho," he begins, rummaging through his man purse and producing his tablet, which I have to come to think of as an extra appendage, "Damon has some things he wants me to discuss with you."

"Fine," I groan as I sink back into Captain's old chair.

"Okay, Damon has decided to wire money to your bank account in the amount of five hundred thousand. He's signed the deed to the penthouse over to you. He wants to pay for your appointments with Dr. Versan for as long as you wish to go," Brian swipes his screen, moving to his next page of notes, I presume.

I am wide-eyed and gaping at what he's just said. Words escape me. He gave me what and what?

"He has also named you as his beneficiary in the event of his death."

The mere thought of Damon dying has my stomach threatening to get me reacquainted with my breakfast burrito. "Don't. Just stop," I plead.

Brian arches his brows at me. "You okay, honey? Want me to grab a trash can?"

I shake my head. "Go tell him that I don't want all of that," I say softly. "I can't. I don't want his money. I want him. Never his money," I reiterate.

"Honey, I know this. But he's just doing what he thinks is the right thing. You know he's just a caveman." Brian shakes his head and I can't help thinking he knows exactly how I feel right now.

I feel like a business transaction. Like an asset that's being liquidated due to issues with demand, not supply.

"He already wired the money, Jo."

I can't even speak. I lean forward and let my head drop onto my desk. Maybe the biggest reason I don't want all of this is because it screams, "It's over!"

"It feels so final," I whimper.

"Sweetheart," Brian coos, scooting over to me. He rubs my back and lays his head on my shoulder. "You're going to be okay. You have me. You have Noni. You still have Grams. You have Andy, who seems like a nice guy. And hot to boot!" He jabs a finger into my side and making me squirm. "I have a meeting in twenty. Are you okay?" Brian asks, stuffing his tablet back into his bag.

"Yeah, yeah. I'll be fine. I've got tons of work to get done so that will keep me busy," I say, looking around at the stacks of papers needing to be sorted. "Hey, is Lindsay still looking for a job?" I ask suddenly.

"Yeah, no luck so far."

"Do you think she'd want to come work here? I wouldn't mind having another person to help with orders, stocking, and inventory, and eventually the store will be open and I can't run the register all the time, so I'll need someone for that too."

"Oh, that would be awesome, Jo!" Brian beams excitedly. "You'd hire her?"

"Yeah. I mean, it's not the best pay, but it's something," I reply with a shrug.

"Have I mentioned how much I love you?" he gushes, pulling me into a hug. "You're a doll. I'll send her over in the morning. Is that okay?"

"Fine by me."

"And I'll email you this information in a bit. Cheer up. I was serious about snotty not being your color." He drops a kiss on my cheek. "Ciao!" He waves on his way out of the office.

*Ciao?* "What? Are you Italiano now?"

"Nope, but I plan on helping myself to one later."

"Oh, God," I groan and lay my weary head back down on my desk. I'm starting to feel really guilty about my snippy attitude with Brian. I owe him so much more than that. I need to practice more restraint. It's just so hard to keep the heartbreak infection from spreading all over me. I'm grumpy and tired and beyond sad. It could be PMS but if I had to stamp a ratio on it, I'd say 90% breakup side effect and 10% PMS.

*PMS?* I pop my head up from my desk and scrunch my brows, thinking hard. My period. I dig for the calendar buried beneath a load of paperwork on my desk. I find the thing and scan it, counting as I go. I flip back one month and another. *Oh hell no.*

I grab Hemingway from his bed and jump from my seat like my butt is on fire. I emerge from the office to see Noni at the cash register, teaching herself every function. She did that yesterday too. I have a passing thought that *she* should train *me* on the register.

"Gotta run. Be back in a bit!" I call as I rush out the door.

# Chapter Thirteen

---

## EMERGENCY

My bathroom is in the same condition as my office and finding my pack of birth control pills proves to be a Herculean task. I need to count pills and days and try to remember the date of my last period. It's a monumental effort on my part. My hands are shaking. My heart is racing. My head is spinning. I need help.

My queasy stomach goes into hyperdrive as I realize there's a very real possibility that I could be... *pregnant. Holy fucking hell.* Instinct has me reaching for my phone. I swipe the screen to unlock it and scroll through my contacts with shaky hands.

I don't have many contacts to speak of, so the scroll through the list is a short one. I make it to the bottom of the list then back up again. "Damon," I mumble. I want nothing more than to call him and insist that he come to the penthouse, but I won't. My pride and dignity are still partially intact and they're all I have to work with at the moment. That, and one skinny jean wearing gay man. I quickly move to Brian's number and click, waiting impatiently for him to answer.

"Hey hey, gorgeous!" he sings into the phone.

"Get your perky ass over here. Pronto. Emergency. Do me a favor and swing by the drugstore. Buy every brand of pregnancy test they sell. Use Damon's money and keep your mouth shut."

"Wai—what? Are you joking right now?" he says, sounding deadpan.

"Not in the slightest, Brianna."

"Jo, I can't. I'm with the boss man right now. Meeting. What would I say?" he asks in a hushed voice, all humor gone.

"Tell him it's a goddamned family emergency!" I whine like a petulant child.

"K, sit tight. Be there in twenty."

We hang up and I sit dazedly on the guest bed for what feels like an eternity. This can't be happening to right now. I'm not pregnant. There's no way. I'm on the pill. I take it at the same time every day without fail.

I begin scrutinizing the last two packs of pills and my responsibility about taking the magic little beasties. One pack was in the bottom of the bag I used before I switched to the one I carry now and the other pack of magic pills was in the drawer of my nightstand beneath my worn copy of *The Catcher In the Rye*. If the locations that I found both of them are any indication, I'm sure that I could have made it a point to be a little more diligent with taking them on time every day. I may have been a little late taking one or two of them but I've never missed a whole day. Hours, yes, but an entire day? No. I could slap myself right now. I'm an idiot. I've been playing with fire where contraception is concerned and I hadn't even realized it. I've been so damn wrapped up in Damon and the store and the new house and wedding plans that don't mean a damn thing now. I cup my head in my hands and do my best the quiet my spinning head and squeamish stomach.

"Jo, baby, where are you?" I hear Brian call out from somewhere in the penthouse.

"In here!" I shout from my perch on the guest bed.

A moment later I hear him scurry down the hall to me. He swings the door open wide, holding two plastic bags from the pharmacy down the street.

"Okay, don't panic! I'm here! This is going to be just fine.

If you're knocked up, you're knocked up. That's fine. Women get preggers every day. Who cares that you and the big guy aren't getting married and now you'll have to be a single mom—"

"Brian!" I shout, sliding off the bed. "Get your shit together. I *may not* be pregnant. It may just be a scare. Like you said, PMS." I hold out my hand expectantly.

He puts the loops of the two bags on my wrist and starts digging into his man purse. Setting the bags down on the bed, I begin ripping open boxes of tests. I'm not even sure how to take these things. I've never been late before.

"This is like an at home chemistry set," I moan, looking over the test strips, droppers, plastic cups and instructional pamphlets.

"Here," Brian says, holding a hand out for the directions for the test in my hand. He flicks the paper open and reads aloud. "Okay, says here that there are two methods for taking the test properly." He skims the bulk of the instructions, mumbling as he goes, and I feel my temperature rise with the bile in my throat. "All right, you can pee on it," he snatches the test stick from my hand and makes a crude visual demonstration that includes him spreading his legs and squatting, "or you can dip it." He tosses the paper down, picks up the plastic cup, and demonstrates that too.

"Oh my God, Brian. What are you, the flight attendant on Pregnancy Test Flight 101 on route to disaster?"

"What?" He shrugs nonchalantly. "I thought a visual would be helpful."

"Gimme this," I snatch the foil-encased test stick and head for the bathroom.

"Pee on it, then come out here for three minutes!" he calls after me. "And don't forget to wash your hands!"

I take a moment to examine myself in the mirror, hoping that this is just a dream or at the very least just a false alarm. Stress can affect your period, right? It could very well be that I've stressed myself into this mess. With one deep breath, I rip open the inanimate plastic stick that isn't really inanimate at all. I swear to God that thing is laughing at me.

I take the test, replace the cap, and wash my hands. I walk out of the bathroom to kill the three minute wait time and see Brian with his ear pressed to his phone and his hands at work on his tablet.

"...no, she just... it's nothing life threatening. W-well, she's not bleeding or anything, actually that's kind of an issue..." he sputters out.

"Ahem!" With my hands planted on my hips, I scowl at my friend from across the guest room.

"Gotta go, Boss." He's quick to hang up. I doubt Damon got a word in edgewise anyway.

"What in the hell are you talking to him for?"

"Jo, he threatened to fire me if I didn't explain this *emergency*," he mocks, making air quotations.

"You didn't tell him anything, right?" I ask with my head slightly cocked to the side.

"No, I just kind of hung up on him." He winces, knowing full well that Damon will have something to say about that later.

I sigh in resignation and plop down on the Queen Anne couch beside him and Hemingway.

"What are your symptoms?" he says conversationally. "The directions say we have three luxurious minutes to chat and I did some googling while you were in there."

"Of course you did," I mutter, fiddling with the hair on the tips of Hemingway's ears.

"Okay, top ten signs of pregnancy," he begins, looking to me. "Missing or late period, check. Frequent urination?"

"Meh," I shrug.

"Tender or swollen breasts? How are your boobs?" Brian reaches over and gives one breast a squeeze.

I wince then bat his hand away.

"Okay, sore boobs, check. What about—"

"Fondling my ex-fiancé was the emergency, Brian?" Damon's deep, smooth voice causes both of us to jump.

We both freeze under his glare. I'm frozen in part because there he is, looking as beautiful as ever, and in part because the cat is about to be let out of the proverbial bag and I know it. *Shit! Shit! Shit!*

"No. Not my scene," Brian admits honestly. *Bless him.*

Damon stuffs his hands into his pockets and keeps his eyes on us as he enters the room. He makes his way to bags on the bed and looks down at the mess of boxes, pamphlets, and various testing paraphernalia. Holding up a box, he looks right through me. I want to die.

"This is the emergency?" His voice is low and velvety and disturbingly calm.

I'm certainly not calm. I don't respond as I get up and walk past him to the bathroom. I shut the door behind me, leaning against the back of it to close my eyes, preparing myself for the verdict. One deep breath in then one out, and I step over to the counter to read the results.

With the test in hand, I reappear, ready to face Damon. I open the door and scan the room for his daunting presence. He's gone.

"He left," Brian explains unnecessarily.

It's a hard, cold, uncaring slap in the face.

"Two lines?" he asks, getting up from his seat and coming right to me.

A nod is the only response I can muster. I'm pregnant with Damon's baby. Under other circumstances, I think I may actually be excited. But this is not good. Brian's sympathetic eyes land on mine. Tears build and swim in my eyes.

Brian wraps me up in a consoling hug. "Oh, honey, don't cry. It isn't the end of the world. Look at Lindsay. My sister is a single mom and she's just fine."

"I don't want it." The words fly out of my mouth. I'm not even sure if I mean them. The guilt is quick and unforgiving. An audible sob escapes my throat and I fall apart on Brian's shoulder. "What am I going to do? He didn't even stay to find out," I cry. The condition I find myself in explains a lot. It explains how emotional I've been lately. It explains the queasy stomach, the heavy, sore breasts, how tired I've been, the snappy attitude. It explains all of it. *Dammit.*

"He told me to let him know the results."

"I don't care," I sniffle, "tell him. He obviously doesn't want to hear the news from me."

# Chapter Fourteen

## BABY CENTRAL

Apparently when a woman finds out that she's pregnant, suddenly it's Baby Central. Every commercial on television has something to do with baby gear or baby food or baby diapers, and every other person you see in public is either pregnant or has a baby on their person.

Case in point: I've popped out of the penthouse two times to walk Hemingway and either I've not noticed before or there is a stroller convention in town because I've seen way too many moms pushing babies or toddlers in strollers that look to be intimidating contraptions meant to confuse adults; they're practically Rubik's cubes on wheels. I saw six—SIX— pregnant women on our walk this morning.

I've spent the last twenty-four hours cooped up in the penthouse stumbling over mounds of clutter and carrying around multiple little plastic sticks that all read "positive" in one shape or form—the actual word, two lines, a plus sign, a smiley face—I took every test Brian brought over and every single one came back the same.

I haven't heard a peep from Damon and it only fuels my disappointment. I know Brian has told him by now. Doesn't he have anything to say? Is he mad? Is he upset? Is he indifferent? It doesn't matter either way because I won't count on an unplanned pregnancy to tie him down to me. I can't think of an unhappier scenario for myself.

Brian rescheduled my meeting with Lindsay for me. I felt bad for not showing this morning, so I promised to be there this afternoon. I check the time on the oven clock and pop another peanut butter cracker in my mouth. I'd better get a move on if I'm going to get showered, dressed and down to the store in time to discuss employment with Lindsay. I inhale the last cracker and gulp down my bottled water.

Hemingway is waiting by the door patiently to be taken outside again. "Okay, okay. Let's go, handsome."

Despite my homely appearance, I walk out into the sunlight, squinting at how bright it is today. Hemingway and I set out on our normal route, stopping for him to mark his usual spots along the way.

Much to my surprise, I see Andy and Chaucer headed my

way. It's early for him to be out. They make long strides, jogging over to us.

"Hey," I greet.

"Hey," he pants as if they've been running.

"What are you doing out here so early?"

"No work today," he explains.

"Oh."

"Jo, you look terrible," he says, touching my elbow. "Is something wrong?"

An uproarious laugh bubbles up in me. I double over, I'm laughing so hard. This is all just so fucked up all I can do is laugh right now. I'm in hysterics. Andy chuckles, looking confused but amused just the same.

"No. I *am* terrible," I sputter through my garbled laughter. I right myself and take a deep breath, sighing. "I'm pregnant."

"What?" Andy chuckles at my outburst then scowls when he realizes I'm serious. "Oh, damn."

"Just found out yesterday. Crazy, huh?"

"Yeah. Wow. Um, does your ex know?" He arches a perfect eyebrow.

"Yeah, he knows," I admit then shrug. "I gotta run to the office for a bit. Catch you later?"

"You got it. See ya."

We walk in the opposite direction. I turn back to look at him. Andy keeps walking away, now with his cell phone pressed to his ear and Chaucer trotting right beside him. *Calling another prospect probably. One that isn't pregnant.*

A hot shower works wonders on the restless. I feel half human again as I walk to my Volvo. I towel dried my hair and splashed on a minimal amount of makeup. Clothes are already proving to be a challenge, though. Along with a shitty binge fest, my pregnant body is plumper than usual, making clothing an entirely new issue. I dug out a flowy shirt to cover the muffin top that I know is spilling over the waistband of my shorts. I feel enormous.

I've managed to estimate that I must be at least six or seven weeks pregnant. It took some pillaging through the pills, a calendar, and some painful memories, but I did it. Damon and I made this baby at a time when we were happy, at least. It's the only upside that I can find to the situation.

I scurry into the store with Hemingway in tow. I'm late. The hilarity of that phrase doesn't completely escape me.

"Sorry I'm late," I announce to Noni and a waiting Lindsay.

"No problem," Lindsay reassures me with a smile.

"How's it going, Noni?"

"I've got it under control." She smiles and holds both

hands up, looking around at her progress with the store.

I examine the full shelves, stocked coffee bar, and remarkably clean store. It's a marvel. "Wow. I guess you do."

Noni smiles, clearly proud of her hard work. I'm so glad she's working here. If it makes her feel more satisfied with life working here than The Diner, then it's all been worth it in my eyes. Noni deserves more than life has handed her. Seeing her happy kind of gives me hope that maybe one day I'll be happy again too.

"Okay, Lindsay, let's go talk. Noni, you too," I wave for both women to follow.

"Me?" Noni squeaks.

"Yes, you." I affirm. "We're a team, you know."

Noni says nothing as she follows Lindsay and I into the office. On the way in I grab the stool behind the cash register and drag it into the tiny office space.

"Okay, so Noni, as store manager, I need your help here."

Her eyes bulge while one hand covers her mouth. "Manager?" she says softly.

"Yep. Manager."

Lindsay smiles sweetly at Noni and I can't help but grin too. Noni jumps from her stool and wraps me up in a hug. Cursed hormones have me fighting back emotion. I love that she's over the moon about her new title.

"Thank you, Jo," she gushes. "Thank you so much."

"Don't thank me. You've earned it. I'd be in trouble without you."

She pulls away from me, swiping a rogue tear on her cheek.

"Okay, enough of that emotional stuff," I begin, then look to both women, who are watching me with a knowing look on their faces.

"Dammit! Brian has a big fat mouth!" I complain, taking my seat at Captain's old desk. I bury my face in my hands, too embarrassed to look at them and positive I'm going to start crying.

"Oh, come on, Jo," Noni says, "everything's going to be fine. A baby is one of the best things in the world."

"I promise it isn't so bad, Jo," Lindsay adds.

I look up to both of them. These women were both dealt shitty hands just like me, but they seem to be doing okay. Noni is practically a new woman these days and Lindsay is the epitome of resilience in the face of adversity. She lost her job and has a beautiful little boy to care for. No men in either of their pictures.

"I don't know if I can keep it," I admit, covering my face in shame again.

Noni purses her lips in sympathy and looks down at her hands. Lindsay just nods. I imagine Brian has given them the whole scoop on Damon and the penthouse and everything.

"Well, you just need to know that I support whatever

decision you make," Noni begins, "but don't let fear make that decision for you. Only your head and heart can make the choice that's right for you. Understand what I mean?"

I sigh. Noni is so good at giving advice, just like Grams. It's how I've always imagined my mom would talk to me if she were still alive. *Oh my God. Does Grams know too?*

"You're so much like me, Jo," Noni continues, taking my hand. "I remember seeing you for the first time and thinking that someone was playing a rotten joke on me or something. You came into that diner with barely any money in your pocket, looking miserable, homeless, and alone, just like I had done so many years before. Now look at yourself." She motions her hand towards the whole of me. "You're a gorgeous, strong, driven, business owner who's expecting her first baby. If you and Damon don't work out, it doesn't change who you are and how far you've come." She pauses and squeezes my hand. "You're still you even if you aren't half of him."

Talking about my failed relationship and unplanned baby tugs at my tender heartstrings. I take in a deep breath and fan my face, trying to keep tears at bay. This is stupid. I never cry this much. Noni and Lindsay both laugh, knowing full well what I am going through.

"I hate hormones," I whine.

It only instigates more laughter from the two woman who inspire me. *I wish Grams was here.* I couldn't help wondering if Damon or Brian were bringing her by to see Noni. I certainly wasn't, since Damon wanted me to keep my distance, but I wouldn't put it past the old broad to make someone else bring her.

"Back to business," I say suddenly, clapping my hands and turning to Lindsay. "Want the job? We're going to need someone to run the register, help customers, and be willing to cover any loose ends that may pop up. Like ordering takeout for lunch." I fake a wide grin, hoping that I've lifted the mood.

Lindsay's eyes widen at my directness but she shakes her head enthusiastically. "Absolutely."

"Want to hire her, Noni?"

Noni looks from me to her then back to me. "Of course," she says with a smile in place.

"Okay, then. Guess you two should get to it, then. Lindsay, Noni will show you around and explain the plans for the store. If you need anything, let me know."

Both women hop up from their seats and hurry back out into the store to do whatever Noni has planned. I'm sure coffee and Danish will be priority, knowing Noni. Food is love in her eyes and she's happy to dole it out to everyone in our screwed up inner circle. It's all she knows. Good food and great advice. And I love her for it.

With so much to think about, I open the browser on my computer and pull up the search engine. I have to decide what the best choice is for me and go for it. It hurts to think of myself ten or twelve years down the road with no Damon and a pre-teen that looks just like him.

It's not a life I think I can endure alone. I have a train wreck of a life and bringing a child into this is just not fair to the baby. What right do I have to screw up this kid's life before they even take their first breath? I need to explore my options and sleep on it. *Adoption? Abortion? Keep him?* I don't have the slightest idea why I would think of the baby as a *he,* it's just kind of the direction my brain went. *He. Him. Baby Damon Cole.*

# Chapter Fifteen

CRAVINGS

About a million and one results come up when I search key terms: pregnancy, abortion, adoption. My mind is swirling. I'm overwhelmed. There's a veritable sea of information out there and I'm just trying to stay afloat.

Adoption seems like a really good option, but I can't help but wonder how hard it would be to give up a baby that I would have carried for nine months. I feel like I would feel a bond with the baby that would be too strong to actually go through with giving *him* up. What if I go through the entire pregnancy preparing myself to sign my child over to adoptive parents and then I back out? I'd feel terrible for doing that to people who are likely very deserving of a child. Then again, what if my baby were to end up being adopted by some monster? I know that adoption agencies are generally very thorough, but you never know. What if I found myself in the nightmare that Noni's negotiating right now—finding out somewhere down the road that someone abused my child and helpless to rectify the situation? There are just too many possibilities.

If I went with adoption, I'd always wonder where my baby was and who he was with and if he was happy and healthy. Adoption scares the shit out of me and makes my heart ache in a completely different way than it aches for Damon.

Abortion doesn't feel any better. In fact, it feels worse. My hand drifts to my stomach instinctively, ready to guard this little human against anything. Against everything. But what if my baby needs guarding from me? What if I'm doomed to wreck everything I touch, including my innocent child? The prospect of that makes abortion sound less scary and more like an option that needs further exploring. How do they abort the baby anyway? What's involved?

I grab a piece of paper and jot down the information to the adoption agency and to a clinic that performs abortions. I'll make my decision tomorrow. Hopefully.

I close the browser and lean back in my seat. I'm so tired.

———— ✺ ————

I'm nearly to my car when I see Damon's BMW come whizzing into the parking lot. He comes screeching to a halt and jumps out before the car is even completely at rest.

His eyes are wild and his breathing labored. "What have you done?" Damon demands, sounding panicked.

*Is he monitoring my browser somehow? Is there a tracking device in my car? How in the world would he have any idea where I was otherwise?* I've never seen him this way. I'm not sure what to say. I look to the clinic then back to him, feeling at a loss for words. I'm instantly ashamed that he's seen me here and must now know what I've been considering as an option for myself and our baby.

"I—" Finding words prove to be more difficult than I'm used to.

"Oh my God. Fuck!" he shouts. "Josephine, you had no right!" The way he's yelling is making me flinch. I look around to see if anyone is watching this embarrassing display. "That is *our* baby. It's *our* decision. Not yours!" he snaps, causing me to bristle.

"What do you care? How did you find me? Go back to whatever slut you're seeing today and leave me alone. It's my body and therefore, my decision," I grate with my finger pointed accusingly at him like a loaded gun.

"Brian told me you were talking about doing this." He motions his hand towards the clinic. "How could you?" He looks defeated. All anger has evaporated and the man before me is beside himself. He looks close to tears.

"Of course Brian told you! His mouth is as leaky as a goddamn sieve. I haven't *done* anything. I just wanted more information, okay?" I admit weakly. I'll choke Brian when I see him. He is the biggest loudmouth I've ever met.

Damon's chest rises as he takes a deep breath—*of relief?* He steps closer to me and pulls me by the arms to the passenger side of his car.

"What are you doing?" I yell.

"We have to talk." Damon looks around as if making sure no one has seen us and it only pisses me off even more.

"Worried Carrie may see us talking?" The bitterness in my voice speaks volumes.

Damon doesn't respond. He just shuts my door and takes determined strides around the front of the car to his side. He slides in and turns the key, bringing the car to life. He takes off into traffic, driving who knows where.

"Where are we going?"

"Somewhere we can talk," he says without even looking at me.

"Um, sure, Damon. I don't mind going with you," I mock his forwardness.

Fifteen minutes later, Damon puts the car in park in front of the house that should have been my home too. It hurts even being here. The first time he took me to see this place was when he proposed. I'd never been happier in my life.

Damon jumps out and skirts the car to let me out. His big hand reaches out toward me. I take it, my hand in his feeling like home. It spawns pure anguish deep in my gut. It hurts so damn much. Being away from him hurts but being so close to him, touching him, is agonizing.

As soon as I'm back to my feet, he releases my hand. I die a little on the inside the moment it's gone. Again. I follow him into the house, where he leads me to the living room and motions for me to sit down.

I settle into the couch and look at him expectantly.

"Listen to me," he orders in a calm voice. "No matter what, don't ever think that I don't want our child. No matter what's going on between you and I, that is my child," he points at my stomach making me feel like I'm under some high voltage spotlight, "and you can't just make decisions with regards to him or her without me." Damon shakes his head disapprovingly. "That isn't right, Josephine."

"I just thought—you acted like you didn't want to have anything to do with me or the baby. You *left* when you knew I had just taken a test, for God's sake! And when I saw you at Ga Tan with Carrie—"

"I wasn't *with* Carrie. She was there with a client. I was

there meeting with Mike. She saw me, came over, and asked where you were. I told her we broke up—"

"No. You broke up with me. There was no *we* to that," I remind him.

Damon rubs the bridge of his perfect nose with his fingers. He's frustrated. "Anyway, I explained that we were no longer together and she helped herself to a seat at our table until I told her to leave."

"You told her to leave?"

"Yes. I had to go make sure that Andy wasn't bedding you in my penthouse. Or bedding you at all for that matter." He mutters the last part mostly to himself, making me wonder if he's just being territorial or if there's any part of him that still thinks of me as his. Stifling that smoldering ember of hope is the only logical thing for me to do. Hope has a way of ripping me apart. I won't indulge in it ever again.

"Andy won't be bedding me at all. Ever. I told him about the baby."

"Who else have you told?"

"No one really. Just him. Brian has blabbed his mouth, though. Noni and Lindsay know too."

"Oh," he says, looking uncomfortable at the mention of Noni's name.

"Have you talked to her?" I ask, careful not to overstep my bounds.

"Yeah," he admits, looking so regretful that I can't help but feel sorry for him.

We may not be together and I may be hurt, but it doesn't change how much I love him. It doesn't automatically shut off my desire to see him happy. It doesn't change the fact that I hate what his father did to all of us.

"I talked to her this morning," I say and make a mental note to stop being so selfish and ask Noni about her talk with Damon and offer her a shoulder if she needs it.

He nods, looking down at his feet. "Good."

This conversation has turned stale quickly. I'm not in charge, though, so I don't know what the hell to say.

"Jo, promise me that you're being careful and taking care of yourself and our baby." Damon steps closer to me and puts his hand on my arm. His touch is just as I have always known it to be, warm and gentle but firm.

I shrug. "I should probably get to the doctor soon, but other than that I'm doing what I guess is the right thing." Damon's hand falls away and I instantly ache for his touch again.

"I'll have Brian make you an appointment with a good doctor," he assures me. "I'll pay for it, of course."

"Right. Okay. Guess I should get back to my car." I have to get out of here. My first instinct is to be pissed about the whole paying for my medical bills thing, but I know that's just Damon and I'm just too overwhelmed to be angry right now.

I'm tired and I have to pee again. Oh yes, and I'm pregnant. My mood doesn't change the affect he has on me, though. It never has. Sitting so close to him is like dangling a pint in front of a recovering alcoholic.

Damon is my drug and I miss him, miss the high that he gives me; being so close to the weakness that I love so much is dangerous. He causes withdrawal symptoms too intense to manage. His scent invades my senses, creeping into my veins, leaving me craving more. I think somewhere in my broken heart is a part of me that hopes that he'll scoop me up like his damsel in distress and beg for me to come home but the practical part of my brain tells me that it's best not to hope so high. I have to stay away as much as I can if I have any chance of healing. I can't cross my fingers and toes that we'll talk this through somehow. Damon isn't much of a talker anyway, especially where his past and his family is concerned. Everything he has ever done in this entire relationship has been in his way in his time. There's no changing that. It's who he is. It's how Damon Cole is wired and I can't let girlish fantasies take over.

# Chapter Sixteen

## Nightmare

I rap on the door three times and wait for Noni to answer. I've only been over a couple of times since she started renting Captain's house. It's still difficult for me to see her stuff in there instead of his, his life pushed aside almost like he didn't exist, even though Noni has been nothing but courteous about his things still being in the house. It's just another reminder that Noni has a heart of gold and that Captain is gone.

I wait at the door with no response from her. *What the hell, Noni?* I fish my cell phone from my back pocket and check to see if I missed a text or phone call from her, but nothing. She told me to come by to discuss some things about the house so here I am. Knowing her, she's likely in the kitchen making fresh coffee and a spread of cookies for me like I'm some special guest or something. That's Noni. Always serving others.

Without giving it much thought, I turn the knob and open the unlocked front door.

"Noni! I'm here!" I call out as I begin making my way towards the living room. I hear a muffled moan followed by heavy, nasal panting coming from the living room and it brings every painful memory of Captain's death racing to the forefront of my mind. "Noni!" I shout as I round the corner into the living room that haunts my dreams, now more so than ever.

The sight before me is straight from a horror flick and I freeze in place just a step inside the room. Noni struggles against the duct tape that holds her captive in one of Captain's dining chairs. My mouth pops open as my eyes bulge and water. Noni jerks in place and cries out from behind the cloth gag stuffed into her mouth. Before my brain can register a response, I feel brute force unleashed on my frame. From somewhere behind me or maybe it's beside me, I'm attacked. It seems like hands and arms are coming from everywhere tugging and pulling at me. A thick hand goes to my mouth and successfully silences my screams. I struggle to wrench myself free from my attacker but another set of hands muscle my arms into submission behind my back. The distinct sound of duct tape being ripped from the roll fills the air around me. My heart feels like it may burst free from my chest. Someone leans in close to my ear and, despite my futile struggle, I feel his breath assault my skin with every syllable he speaks.

"Don't fight me," he warns.

My blood runs subzero cold when I realize that he's here. It's him and it's the first time since the accident that I feel completely vulnerable to the monster that wrecked my world. I'm at his mercy and so is my baby.

The tape is wrapped tight, making my fingers feel plump with blood and slightly numb. A piece of cloth that tastes chalky with dust is crammed into my mouth despite how hard I clench my jaw shut. It's pried open and in the disgusting cloth goes. I look around frantically but I can't see whoever is behind me. I know Edward is here, but paralyzing shock crashes over me when I'm whirled around and dragged to a chair beside Noni.

Howard. Andy. Andy was the one stealing checks from Grams' room at the retirement home—that's the reason he was always the one to fix shit for her and why he was so cozy with both of us. This is the only reason he pursued me. That son of a bitch.

Seeing Howard mixed up in all of this is surprising, though. He's the Head of Security at the penthouse and one of Damon's inner circle. He trusted him. I trusted him.

"Worthless piece of shit!" I grind out from behind the cloth in my mouth.

Edward motions Howard to his side and he heels like a well-trained bird dog. "Strap her down," Edward orders and I watch Howard crouch beside me with nylon rope in hand.

"I'm sorry, Miss Josephine, I don't have a choice. I need the money," Howard apologizes, looking like a cowering animal.

"Fuck you!" I growl, sure that even with a gag in my mouth, my words ring clear. I lunge at him; Howard flinches and falls back on his ass. It's a small victory.

A powerful blow explodes against my cheek so hard that I see fluorescent shades of yellow, green, and pink. My vision is splotchy for a long moment before it begins to clear. My head feels heavy and lolls to one side. Warmth trickles down my cheek coming from what I assume must be a gash. I hear Noni's subdued cries beside me and try my best not to cry. Fucking hormones and pain.

The distinct, metallic taste of blood floods my mouth. A reflexive inspection with my tongue finds all my teeth still in place but my upper molars have sliced a fair-sized cut on the inside of my cheek. A heartbeat grows to epic proportion on the left side of my face, bringing swelling and more blood with it. I have no choice but to swallow the blood in my mouth down or choke on it, so I focus on swallowing and trying not to vomit as it seeps out. My skin begins to feel tight as the swelling causes my flesh to expand.

In the time that it takes for me to gather cognitive thought, Howard has secured my legs to the chair and Handy Andy has proven just how handy he is by binding my arms to the back of the chair. I turn my head to see that I mirror Noni exactly. Bound, gagged, and bleeding. We look like a matching pair except for one thing—Noni has a look of complete fear on her sweet face and I'm pissed.

I'm fighting mad and I want nothing more than to take a bat to these worthless motherfuckers in no particular order! The instinct to fight that I cultivated within myself when I was a kid rears its brazen head and I go with it. I'll kill all of them if I get the chance. I'll slice them from nuts to neck with the dullest knife I can find. Like a woman possessed, I eye each of them individually, unafraid of the physical abuse that I'm sure they're happy to dole out. I'll take it. I'll take it all because anger is what will see me through this the same way it saw me through all these years without Maman and Papa. Anger will drive me forward. Anger will save me and maybe Noni too. I may end up in some shallow grave in the desert soon but, dammit, I'll fight every second until I can't fight any longer.

"Pretty nice house that old fucker left you, Josephine," Edward taunts as he takes his seat across from Noni and me. He's maybe three feet in front of us, conveniently within arm's reach.

I jerk and pull against the ties that bind me, hoping at least one of those losers sucks at knot tying. Edward's half lit and chuckles like the pig that he is.

"Fuck you!" I scream.

It's clear that he's heard my insult, because he jumps to his feet, draws back and hammers his balled fist into my face. It's unclear where he's hit me, because my entire head spins in pain. It's excruciating. Pain reverberates throughout me. Blood gushes into my mouth and I quickly swallow it down. My nostrils flare as I try to catch my breath. It's so hard to breathe like this. You don't realize it until you're forced into it.

Noni's desperate cries get louder as I try to stifle down the pain that his assault has brought on. Hearing Noni's cries caused by the man who has tormented her so much makes me wish for super-human strength. I want to rip free from this chair and get her out of here. I want to protect her from the monster standing in front of us. Her frightened cries only feed my desperation to get us out of this mess.

"Say it again, bitch! I dare you," Edward grinds out just inches from my face.

The scent of booze, generally bad breath, and tobacco is enough to make anyone vomit. I groan and turn my head to avoid the stench. His bloodshot blue eyes are the darkest I've ever seen. Something evil dwells within this man and I'm sure it's something that he comes by naturally. There's no way that

Grams had any hand in this. She couldn't have raised such a monster.

"You know, Jo, you'd be surprised what I know about you," he comments, poking me in the forehead with his dirty finger, his pronounced gut shaking heartily with his laughter. "Wanna know what I know?"

I begin to shake my head no but I think better of it as soon as the movement has my head hurting so much worse. Instead of responding, I look to Noni. I focus hard on her and pray for some brilliant escape plan to hit my foggy brain.

"I know who you are," he whispers conspiratorially. "I know that you were dead broke before you got all cozy with my idiot son and senile mother and now you're a spoiled little twat. You've turned my own mother against me!" He yells the last part, spittle flying into my face, the boom of his voice making my developing headache that much more painful. "And then *this*," he motions to Noni, "this is just wonderful. You can't imagine my enthusiasm when I realized that you *just so happened* to track down this bitch."

I watch Noni and see her cringe under his verbal assault. God, I wish he had left her alone. I didn't mean to get her dragged into whatever mess this has turned out to be. I can't imagine what in Edward's fucked up head makes him think that I had anything to do with whatever misfortune he's been met with. In actuality, I'm sure he's just dug himself in too deep and sees no way out. He's an irrational drunk with a serious skill for blaming other people for his screwed up life.

"I've told you a few things, so what do you have to tell me?" With one swift jerk, he's pulled the gag from my mouth.

I lick my lips and moisten my mouth once the rag is gone. "What do you want to know?" I force out hoarsely.

"I need to know where the money is."

"What money?"

"My mother's money!"

"I-I don't know. I don't have anything to do with that." My mind is racing so fast it's difficult to keep things clear. I don't know what money he's talking about. The blood trickling from somewhere above my eyebrow has leaked into my eye and dried a bit. It makes blinking feel sticky. It's a distraction. I don't recall Damon or Grams telling me anything about the missing money or what was going to become of Grams' remaining money. Damon said he was going to take care of it and I left it at that. It's never any use trying to meddle in business matters where Damon is concerned. He doesn't say much about business stuff and his take on the missing money was definitely all business.

"Don't fuckin' lie to me! I know you know!"

"Stop!" I scream. "Let me fucking think," I say, trying to bide my time to figure out what the hell he's talking about... *Grams' money, Grams' money. Where is it?* "The last I heard of it, Damon was handling Grams' accounts after he found out that some money was going missing."

Realization plows through my aching brain. *Andy!*

Before thinking any better of it, my eyes find Andy leaning against the wall behind Edward, eating from a can of mixed nuts like he's just hanging out at a bar, shootin' the shit. Bastard.

"You!" I accuse.

He shrugs casually. "Me," he supplies with a wink.

"You pretended to be my friend! You tried to—you wanted to fuck me, you—you bastard!" It isn't much of an insult, but it's the most dominating of my thoughts. I feel ill remembering his mouth covering mine in front of the penthouse the night I went with him to Ga Tan.

Andy shrugs and snickers, tossing another fistful of Noni's food into his rotten mouth.

"He's going to kill all of you," I hiss.

My eyes dart to Howard, who's sitting in a chair by the front windows, no doubt keeping an eye out. He turns to face me when he hears my warning. The worried look in his eyes tells me he knows that Damon was the wrong man to mess with. His eyes meet Edward's steely glare and he returns to his lookout duties.

"Howard, he may kill you first," I warn, "simply because he trusted you."

I face forward again to see Edward motion to Andy and I know that I've likely just earned myself more pain. Handy Andy abandons his snack on Captain's side table and scurries over like the obedient little worker that he is. His hands go to my jaw and I don't resist. I let him pry my mouth open while Edward takes another long pull of amber-colored liquor then stuffs the bloody rag back into my mouth.

Edward smirks, making my heart seize in my chest. "*Damon* won't be doing a damn thing to anyone."

*What's that supposed to mean? Where's Damon? What are they going to do to him?*

Noni's soft cries pull my attention from Edward to her and all at once I feel like the only person in the room that doesn't know something. Something important. Thoughts of my Big Man flood my mind. Along with thoughts of Damon come thoughts of the baby I'm carrying. Damon's baby.

"You know, you look very nice with your mouth open, Jo." Andy drags his index finger across my jaw, forcing me to jerk away beneath his unwelcome touch and cut my eyes up at him, hoping he gets the message I'm sending. "I'd still like to sample what's under those clothes," he croons, his voice repulsively sincere.

"Andy, we gotta talk." Edward summons Andy to Captain's kitchen, leaving Howard to watch Noni and me.

The moment they've left the room I lock eyes with Howard, sending him a silent request. His eyes drift away from us, as if it's too difficult to look at the scene before him.

"Howard," I muffle. "Help us," I go on, hoping he can discern my simple plea. "Don't do this."

He closes his eyes tight and drops his head. He knows better than anyone that whatever amount of money he's being paid, whatever compensation he's been offered, it won't be nearly enough payment for what Damon will do to all three of them. "I'm sorry," he mutters weakly, then turns his attention back to peeking out of the window blinds. The rational part of my brain knows that he must be doing this for the medication that he said his father needed, but the pissed off part of my brain wants to bludgeon his skull for being such a traitorous sellout.

Edward reenters the room with Andy in tow, cracking his knuckles like he's a big dog.

"Here's the deal, bitch," Edward growls, jerking the gag from my mouth, "I need money. I owe some serious dough to some people that are dangerous like you couldn't even read about. I was on my way to paying my debt when suddenly, my access to money was cut off. Now I have no choice but to squeeze money from that asshole son of mine to fund my life in Mexico. The only thing that makes you worth a damn is your 'condition.' He may have ditched you, but lucky for me, you got knocked up, making you a very valuable person to my son. He's always been a pussy."

My eyes widen. Andy told him. I see where all of this is going now and it's the worst case scenario besides being murdered, I guess. They want money, loads of it from what I can tell, and they're using me and this baby as a bargaining chip. *How is this happening right now?* This shit only happens in the movies. No one gets kidnapped for ransom in real life. People just kill other people and try their best to escape the police. He's not going to let us go. He wouldn't tell me details about his plan if he planned on letting me go. They've made no effort of hiding their identities or disguising their voices. They don't intend on allowing us to live. *No witnesses.*

"You can go to hell!" I snarl, then spit right in his disgusting face. Had I thought better of it, I probably wouldn't have done that simply because I know I've just earned out quite a beating; a beating that will put my child at risk. I can't afford to be reckless where my baby is concerned.

Edward pulls a hanky from his back pocket and wipes his face. "You'll pay for that shortly," he warns, his voice even so I know he's sincere. "So, here's the plan," he continues, grabbing onto my hair to make me meet his eyes, "you're going to call Damon and have him come over just like we had her call you." He nods to Noni with a disgusting leer. "Make something up. Just get him here."

"Okay," I concede. My mind is racing a million miles per hour. I've got to say something that will let him know something's not right. *Think, Jo. Think.*

Edward nods to Andy, who locates my cell phone within what I swear is seconds and dials Damon. He thrusts the phone at me, holding it in place so that I can pin it between my throbbing head and shoulder.

Damon answers on the third ring. "Hello."

"Hey," I begin in the steadiest voice I can muster.

"Josephine?"

Hearing him say my name makes me ache. The territory of my heart is fragile. Knowing that I'm about to lure him into this mess gives me pause. I don't want him to get hurt. I don't want something terrible to happen. He may not want me anymore, but I still love him, maybe more now than ever. I have to protect him.

"Hey, I was wondering something," I continue.

"Yes?" He sounds puzzled, but I hope to clear the fog with what I have to say.

"Remember what you promised me that night in bed? The first night after Grams moved in?"

He sighs, obviously recalling the moment we shared. "Yeah."

"I need you to make good on that promise. I'm stuck at Captain's house. My car is doing something weird. Can you fix it?"

"What's going on?" His voice has deepened and I can hear shuffling from his end of the line. He's already on the move.

"Um, I don't know what's wrong with this thing. I just know I can't fix it on my own, so come prepared, okay?"

"If something's wrong, say anything other than no."

"Yeah, Noni's here," I answer conversationally.

"It's him isn't it?" I can hear a loud crashing noise, which was likely Damon's fist meeting some poor door or desk.

"Right. Okay, see you in a few," I chime, feigning a cool and calm demeanor.

Andy ends the call before I can say anything else and takes the gag from my lap, shoving it back into my mouth. He slips my cell phone back into his pocket and runs the backs of his filthy fingers over my face, making a condescending "tsk tsk" when his knuckles graze beneath the gash on my forehead.

Edward is all business as soon as he knows Damon is on his way, and it makes me even angrier and a helluva lot more anxious. "Howard, make sure you can't be seen from that window," he barks. "Andy, stand in the foyer so that the door blocks you when he comes in. That'll put you behind him. I'll hang back in here. Now once he's down, we've got to move fast. Got it?"

Both men agree to do as Edward ordered, but I'm stuck on "once he's down." *What does he mean, once he's down?* A painful knot builds in my gut, knowing that Damon is coming here to be ambushed by these dipshits. He's putting himself at risk for me and Noni and our child. I can't stomach the thought of something happening to Damon. I won't be able live with myself if something happens to him.

What feels like an eternity passes and then there's a

knock at the door. Noni whimpers. Tears stream down her face. She's just as scared as I am. I hear the door open. Footsteps knock against the floor and I wait for disaster.

"Jo, babes, where are you?" Brian calls out, not sounding like himself.

*He knows.* Damon must have told him that something was going on. My dear friend is so brave coming here; he's just walked into a nightmare for me.

"Damon sent me to get this thing towed," he yells, still at the door. "Did you call AAA already?"

*Where's Damon? Oh, God, Damon. Where are you?*

The door shuts with a slam and we heard rustling, then a loud thud. "Brian!" I scream through the fucking stupid gag. Noni's cries turn frantic. I look to her to see her staring at Edward. He's got a gun drawn and pointed at the entrance to the living room.

"Shut up, bitch!" Edward growls, waving the pistol into the air. He brings the butt of the gun down hard against Noni's head and she instantly goes limp.

Andy appears in the arched entrance of the living room with Brian, weakened but still struggling against him. "Just him," he grunts.

"Fuck!" Edward shouts.

"What now?" Andy asks, holding Brian in a sort of hand on hand combative hold. Both of Brian's arms are locked with Andy's and hoisted upward, forcing his shoulders downward submissively. In that awkward position, small-framed Brian is just as immobile as I am in this chair.

Brian's has one bloodied eye but he sees me. He fights hard against Andy, trying to break his hold. My emotion gets the best of me seeing my friends beaten and bloodied and I finally start to cry. My sobs make breathing through my nose so much harder. I feel so lightheaded. I tug at my bonds. I need to break free. I need to help Brian.

I make eye contact with Brian and he winks back, fixing his eyes on me with a brave, determined smile. He rears back one foot and brings it crashing into Andy's knee. Andy yelps like a wounded animal and his hold on Brian loosens enough for Brian to jerk away, freeing one arm. They struggle and Brian goes for the front door with Andy after him. A deafening blast rings out, making my ears useless. My eyes instinctively squeeze shut. All I can hear is ringing. My eyes pop open to see Brian squirming on the floor. He's shot. Blood is pouring from his leg or maybe it's his gut. It's difficult to tell. I pull against the chair and scream as loud as I can, but I'm useless. There's no way for me to help my friend. Brian inches, belly down, towards the foyer. He's groaning gutturally. One side of his body is limp, leaving the other side to do all of the work to escape and though I know it's not possible for him to make it past the door, my heart clenches in my chest hoping that somehow he will.

This whole situation has spun out of control fast. I look to

Edward, who's scrambling after Brian. Andy, who had dropped when the shot was fired, gets to his feet and grabs one of Brian's ankles. Edward grabs the other and together they drag Brian back from the door, flailing weakly and groaning in agony.

"Let him go!"

I'm unsure if my ears have failed me or if I'm delirious and imagining things, but my eyes find him standing in the adjacent dining room with a gun drawn, aimed at Edward. Damon doesn't take his eyes off Andy and Edward. That fucker, Edward, rights himself and whirls around to face Damon, his own gun in hand. Howard remains by the window with his hands raised in surrender.

"Step away from him," Damon demands.

"Fuck you, you prick!" Edward spits.

Everything has happened so fast. My head is spinning and I'm terrified. It's hard to believe that Damon is really here. He's here and he has a gun. He's come to save us. Everything has happened so fast. My brain battles to keep grip on reality. I want to close my eyes and wish it all away.

"I want my money," Edward bites out, shaking his gun a little.

"The police are already on their way." Damon's gaze goes to Howard, then to Andy, his voice is calculated and calm. "Go ahead and run. Run fast and far, because I'm going to find you, and when I do, I'm going to kill you."

It's all the warning Howard needs. He takes one look at Edward then Andy and bolts fast for the front door. Andy nods to Edward and follows suit. He takes off running like a man on fire. I hope they don't get far. They can't. The police have got to catch them. They should be here by now. *Where are they?*

"Get back here!" Edward demands.

It's just him and Damon now. I watch helplessly as Edward trains the barrel of his gun on Damon's head. *Oh, God. He's going to kill his own son.*

"Money! Get on the phone right now and have a quarter million wired to my account," he screams. "I want the money that I'm owed!"

"Haven't you taken enough?" Damon responds.

I hear the double meaning behind Damon's rhetorical question. He couldn't be more right. Edward has taken so much from everyone in this room. He stole Noni's innocence and aspirations. He stole Damon's entire adolescence. He stole my family. His mother's money is nothing in comparison.

Sirens in the distance ring out, drawing nearer by the second. Edward looks frantic and desperate, his hands starting to shake on the gun. He's out of options. This hasn't gone the way he had planned and all is lost. There's no possible way that Damon could get him any substantial amount of money right now, even if he was inclined to.

Edward lost and he knows it.

His hand grows even more unsteady the louder the sirens become. "You've always been a worthless little fuck," Edward spits.

The scene before me nearly comes to a standstill, playing out in slow motion, frame by frame. I'm forced to watch as Edward's grasp tightens around the grip of his pistol and his aim becomes steady. I close my eyes and prepare for the worst. Another deafening blast resonates throughout the house. The sulfuric scent of burnt gunpowder permeates my sinuses, driving home the realization of what's just happened.

It's against my better judgment, or maybe it's because of my natural tendency for self-loathing antipathy, but I open my eyes and look to find Damon lying on the floor.

But he isn't.

He's standing right where he was, his gun still drawn. He looks down, examining himself for wounds. He's not bleeding. He's not shot. He's there, alive and well and I couldn't feel a bigger sense of relief.

Edward is on his back right where he stood with a growing pool of blood flowing from his head. He's dead. Damon shot and killed his own father. The monster that tormented Damon from birth is now lifeless on the floor.

The sounds of sirens and screeching tires followed by what must be twenty pounding feet rushing through the house drag my attention to the entrance to the living room.

"Drop your weapon!" multiple police officers demand.

Damon crouches slowly and sets his pistol on the tiled floor. Policemen move in fast and scurry around, some to Brian, some to Edward, some to Noni. There must be someone near me, but all I can focus on are the two men forcing my Big Man to the ground.

Damon doesn't fight them. He complies, pressing his cheek against the floor, his eyes facing me. My gaze meets his and I fear the vacant look he wears is a sign that this has ruined him forever.

# Chapter Seventeen

## FREE

I think the worst thing about all of this is the feeling of being robbed. I had the store all these years and it was my foundation, my rock. I had been managing at least mostly okay without Captain because the store was my real lifeline in a world that seemed ready to swallow me up given half the chance. Now I have to let it go just like I have to let Damon go. The idea of giving up both is a devastating blow to my already wounded heart.

Twelve days ago, I watched from a stretcher as Damon was cuffed and hauled away in the back of a police cruiser. The media coverage has been nearly constant. While no charges have been brought against Damon, he has still been under close scrutiny by law enforcement and pushy reporters.

Brian was taken to the hospital, where he underwent surgery to remove the slug from his upper thigh. The doctors said he was lucky to have been shot there and not two inches to the left, else he would have bled out. He's been in good spirits about it all though. Trey thinks it's cool that his uncle is a hero. Lindsay was worried sick over the whole ordeal. She's been by his side nonstop. Brian went on about how his current exploit would "dig" the scar too. I've only visited him once because seeing him any more than that would make doing what I have to do that much more difficult. I think he still has another week to go before they discharge him.

Noni suffered a concussion thanks to the butt of Edward's semi-automatic, but she's recovering well with the help of Grams. She insisted that Noni stay on her sofa bed while she recovered. I can understand Grams' need to take care of the woman who gave her Damon 33 years ago.

When the paramedics began checking me out, reality struck hard. I worried that something would be wrong with my baby. I worried that I would lose him or her and the idea was more than I could handle. The ultrasound probe revealed my baby's strong steady heartbeat from within the safety of my womb. There it was, in the shape of a tiny person, making little movements that I couldn't really feel, completely unaware of the chaos on the outside. When the doctor reassured me that the baby was fine, I think I took the first deep breath I had in weeks. Seeing my little angel on that screen made things so clear for me. I knew right then that I'd do anything for this baby. I'd keep him or her safe from harm. I'd even walk away from the only city that I have ever called home. I left the hospital only a few hours after I was brought there with a plan in place. I went back to the penthouse and got to it.

My heart aches so much I find it hard to breathe sometimes. My nights still consist of waking up off and on to the sound of my own crying, but none of that ache changes the bottom line and that bottom line is that I have to leave Las Vegas. I have to make a new life for myself and my baby. Alone. I know now how frightened seventeen-year-old Noni must have been facing the world alone with a baby on the way. At least I'm an adult with some sort of skill set... though I'm not sure reading and a being a smartass will get me many job prospects.

It makes me think of Maman and Papa and how scared they must have been to start all over in a new place—a new country with a different language and everything. What they did inspires me. It shows me that I can do this. I can be strong and courageous; if not for myself, then for my child. It's amazing that someone so tiny, someone who hasn't even been brought into this world, is powerful enough to change my life so completely.

If I'm being honest, I knew from the beginning that a life with Damon was doomed for failure, but it doesn't make my heart hurt any less. I've lost Captain, I've forfeited the store, I've lost Damon, I've lost the future I envisioned for myself. I've forfeited Grams, and Noni, and Brian. When I really think about it, all three of them belong to Damon, and instead of making them pick sides, I left them for him. He needs the support and I don't need any strings. Like a coward, I changed my cell phone number to avoid the painful conversation. A clean break is best, right?

There is beauty in my situation, though. I'm free. I'm free from a past that has been a formidable opponent for far too many years. I'm free from constant reminders that bring back memories too painful to endure. I'm free from news coverage about Damon. I'm free from probing reporters. I'm free from the life that I had here. Vegas is a tumultuous ride that I'm ready to get off of.

One last stop and I'm ready to get on the road. The cemetery comes into view and I wait for the feeling of encompassing dread that visiting this place brings. I kill the engine and get out to make my way over to Maman, Papa, and Captain's plots. I keep my eyes on my feet as I go. It's still so hard to see those headstones knowing what they represent, the lives and deaths of three people that mean so much to me.

I get to my knees, resting my backside on my feet behind me. "Hey." It's the only word that comes out even though I have so much to say, so much to confess, so much to promise.

I clear my throat and try to gather my thoughts. "I have to

say goodbye for now," I croak, trying hard to keep my emotions under control. They may be gone but I feel like they're right here with me. I hope that they are. "I, uh... turns out I'm moving to Salt Lake City. It's not too far for me to drive here and visit a few times a year. Damon will still be able to have a relationship with the baby. I know what you're thinking, Captain. I know it's not exactly my type of place, but I'll make it work. I have to, with the baby coming and all." My hand goes to my small belly and I smile a little. "It's going to be a great place for us to start over." I look from one stone to another to another. "I just wanted to stop by and say that I-I love you. All of you—" A sob breaks through my paper thin resolve. "And I miss you so, so much. I wish you all were here. I'm scared to raise this baby alone..."

"You don't have to be."

I shoot to my feet, nearly falling over as I do. Damon jumps forward, steadying me. *His hands*. His hands are warm and supportive against my arms.

"What are you doing here?" I ask, swiping tears from my cheeks and chin. I fiddle with my shirt, straightening the hem nervously.

Damon wraps his fingers around my elbow and leads me back to my Volvo. I don't see his truck or car anywhere. "Where's your car?"

He shakes his head. "Mike dropped me off at the gate. I walked in."

"Stop and listen to me for just a minute. Please. Give me two minutes, Jo." His eyes are so warm and pleading that it does something to my insides and I relent, crossing my arms over my chest but listening to him nonetheless. "You don't have to leave. I don't want you to go."

"It's already done, Damon," I say quietly. "I have a place waiting for me. You haven't called. I haven't seen you. Nothing has changed."

"So cancel it."

"Did you not hear me? It's not just the new place. Don't you understand?" I sound exasperated because I am. I can't go through all of this again. I can't give myself false hope again. I don't have it in me to rescue him again. This relationship will never work and I'm trying hard to come to terms with that. My heart can't afford any more abuse.

"I'll fix all of it." Damon lifts his hand to cup my cheek. His touch is tender and I melt a little on the spot. "Let me fix it, baby," he pleads. "Please come home."

I look up into those warm eyes that have entranced me since the first time I saw him. His tears glisten in the sunlight. It's so hard to see him this way.

"Damon—"

"Please," he urges, stepping closer to me.

"I'm scared," I admit.

"You don't have to be scared. I never wanted to hurt you. I love you. I was trying to protect you and things got out of control. I never wanted to lose you, or the baby." One hand drops from my face to my small, pregnant belly.

"But you—"

"I know." He looks at his feet, his guilt evident in the stoop of his shoulders, and then back up to me with a sigh. "The day that I told you to leave was the day that Mike gave me his report. My father was becoming desperate and Mike felt that something bad was in the works. We just couldn't pin it down. He advised me to keep you safe, Josephine. It nearly killed me seeing you heartbroken because of a lie, but I had no choice. I had to try to keep him away from you and I thought that if you weren't a part of my life, he'd leave you alone."

"You should have told me!" I cry, balling up my fist and hammering it into his muscular chest. "Why haven't you told me this until now?"

"I couldn't risk it. I know how stubborn you are. I was trying to protect you, truly." He grabs my fist and holds in tightly in his hand. "I know you, love. You wouldn't have given up. You wouldn't have left unless I convinced you that I didn't want you. I've tried to let the media coverage cool down before getting you caught up in all of it again, but I couldn't wait any longer. I couldn't let you leave town."

"But the baby! You acted like you barely cared," I accuse, tears threatening.

"I do care. Of course I care. Do you know how hard it was

for me to walk out of the penthouse that day you found out?" His tears begin to fall and he does nothing to wipe them away. "Do you know how badly I wanted to stay with you? To celebrate? I left there and hoped and prayed that Brian would call to let me know that the test was positive. When he did, I knew I had to see this through. You're having my child, Jo. My baby. I had to keep him away from my family."

I'm speechless and confused and relieved and angry.

"I want nothing more than to make babies with you. Lots of them, if you want. I want you to marry me. I want to go through life with you by my side, Jo. I wanted that test to be positive because I knew if you were already pregnant that I may have a better chance of winning you back, a better chance of reversing all of this."

I hide my face in my hands as the flood gates burst open. My heart can't take much more of this. I came here to say goodbye, yet here I stand, wrapped in Damon's embrace, being told that I was scammed.

That none of that was real.

That it was all a ploy. A means to an end. Edward's end.

"Please don't cry, baby." Damon leans down, pressing me to his chest, and drops tender kisses against the shell of my ear. "Please don't cry."

"I-I... you ripped my heart out!" I accuse him, still wrapped up in his arms.

"I know. I'm so sorry. You have no idea how sorry I am.

Let me make it right, Jo." Damon's hands grip me by my shoulders and hold me at arm's length. One big paw reaches into his shirt pocket and retrieves my ring, glittering and sparkling in the sunlight. He lifts my left hand to him. "Please come home," he urges, slipping the ring back into place on my finger.

I watch in silence as he gets down to his knees. With one tentative look up at me, he slips one hand under my shirt, resting it against my barely swelling belly. His eyes close and he leans his forehead against my abdomen. He's trying to make amends. He's showing his cards. It's clear that Damon wants our baby just as much as I do. And he wants me too.

I can feel his thumb making slow strokes against my belly. Seeing him like this, so tender, makes me melt. It breaks my heart knowing that he did all of that lying and planning and risking because he loves me and our baby that much. He risked so much to keep us safe. He was willing to lose me if it meant I could be safe. It reminds me of that first night when we moved Grams into her apartment. He made love to me and asked if I knew that he'd always keep me safe, no matter what. I knew then just like I know now.

I tug on his arms urging him to stand. "Jo, baby, say you'll come home. Say you'll still marry me." His eyes are pained, worry lines mar his handsome face, and I can't take another moment of it.

"Yes and yes." My answer is simple but heavy with the

promise of a second chance. "On one condition," I go on. "Noni. She has to be a part of this baby's life. I love her and I know you do too. Somewhere in here," I press my palm to his chest, over his heart, "you love her too. You've been hurt but it's time to make amends."

"I know. I will," he promises, raining kisses onto my face. "I'm not mad at her. It wasn't her fault. She's my mother and there's a lot we have to talk about but I'll do it. I'll do anything you want. I love you. You don't know how happy you've just made me."

In one swoop, I'm gathered up against my Big Man's chest and reveling in the feeling of peace. Being in his arms is home for me. I'm so glad to be home again.

# Epilogue

## THREE MONTHS LATER...

I examine my reflection in the mirror one more time. My makeup is as good as it's going to get. My eyes are rimmed in a smoky black eyeliner and my eyelashes look the longest and fullest they've ever looked, thanks to the hormones that I disliked so much at the beginning of my pregnancy. My lips are pouty and painted with a natural dark pink gloss. The pearls that Grams gave me are in place around my neck and wrist. They're my "something old" and they couldn't be more perfect. Noni offered to do my hair and I'm beginning to think that she's a Jill of all trades. My hair falls down my back in big soft curls in a sort of 1920s glamorous style. She pinned back a few soft curls with her favorite silver hair comb, incidentally taking care of my "something borrowed." Brian nearly fainted when I told him that we would be marrying in typical Vegas style in a wedding chapel. I know he was looking forward to the meticulous wedding planning details, and I may have burst his fashionista bubble, but keeping our nuptials private and intimate is the only way to keep the media out of all of it. The bulk of news coverage about the kidnapping and subsequent death of Edward has decreased to a trickle, but reporters still linger around waiting for any opportunity to question us.

Mike's report ended up being eerily accurate. Edward was in deep with a few different high end bookies here in town. He was desperate for money and drowning in alcoholism and debt. Andy and Howard were brought in mere days after the incident and are both awaiting trial on charges a mile long. Howard is the one who gave the most information, agreeing to testify about Andy's involvement in the whole thing. Reportedly, Edward had planned on coercing Damon out of a substantial amount of money and then fleeing the country, but Damon and I already knew that...

Grams took Edward's death hard. He was a sick bastard, but he was still her son. I think most of her mourning has been out of sheer regret that she couldn't convince him to be the man she'd hoped he would be. I can respect that. I feel terrible for Grams; she's just as much a victim in this disaster as the rest of us. Grams has basically adopted Noni. They're both living in Grams' apartment and working side by side at the store every day. Grams keeps Noni company and entertains the younger crowd in the coffee bar with her stories and antics. I can't blame Noni for not wanting to go back to Captain's house. I don't want to go there either. I was holding onto it because I was scared to forget Captain, but Dr. Versan has helped me see that Captain's memories are as alive and vivid as I want them to be. I don't have to keep his house to keep my memories of him. The house has been up for sale for two months. No luck selling it yet. Prospective buyers aren't too impressed with its history. Elise was shocked and devastated, of course, to find out that her father had been shot by her brother. She wasn't angry though. She was sad, but happy that no one else was fatally wounded. She came right to Damon as soon as she was notified of the shooting and she's been supportive of both of us. Damon didn't say much, of course, but I know he was relieved that Elise didn't make him feel guilty for killing their father and I love her for that. She handled all of Edward's funeral arrangements and moved nearly all of his belongings into her garage on the other side of town so that neither Grams nor Damon would have to go through his things.

"You ready yet?" Brian peeks his head into the dressing room.

"Yep. I think so," I say, giving my silent approval to my reflection with Noni and Grams, the two most important women in my life, both flanking me, smiling and giving their approval as well.

"Damon wanted me to give this to you," Brian says, handing me a small velvet box.

I smile wide, thinking about how sweet my Big Man can be. The box opens with a creak and I gasp.

Maman's watch. It's back in my possession and ticking strong and steady. I pull it from the box and flip it over. There it is, in my family's native French.

### *Collette, mon coeur reside avec vous pour toujours plus*

"Collette, my heart resides with you, forevermore," I whisper the translated phrase to myself.

Something about this watch reminds me of my relationship with Damon. It has seen so much. It has been worn and damaged. It didn't work for a while, but with expert attention, here it is, ticking along like it never stopped. And beneath the beautiful veneer is the heart of it all.

"My heart resides with you, forevermore," I croak out again, unable to keep my tears at bay.

"Oh, honey, no crying," Brian chastises gently.

"I can't help it. It's so perfect. He's so perfect."

"Okay, that's a stretch, honey," Brian jibes, fastening the watch on my wrist and taking my hand. "Let's get you hitched."

I smile at my best friend and the realization that I'm about to marry the man that I was made for hits me. Tragedy may have surrounded our existence for so long, but it brought us together; clinging to that truth makes accepting those tragedies that much easier.

We go to leave the dressing room with Grams and Noni in tow, but I freeze, stepping back over to the vanity counter for my "something new" which also happens to be my "something blue." A teeny tiny blue baby sock. I grab my bouquet of calla lilies from Brian and carefully stuff the tiny sock into the center of the flowers beneath the blooms. Our sweet baby boy will be here in four short months, but I wanted to include him in our wedding. This is my way of doing just that.

"There," I say confidently. "Now I'm ready."

I watch with a smile as Brian takes his place at the altar as my "Man of Honor" next to Damon and Mike Passarelli. Damon asked Mike to be stand up for him since we owe him so much. He's the reason Damon was able to take the steps necessary to protect me and our unborn child. He stood guard, watching every move that Edward made, prepared to act if the time came. Mike was persistent and convinced Damon that the best thing he could do was stage our breakup, making me less of a target. Damon had no way of knowing that my pregnancy not only made me a target in Edward's eyes, it made me the perfect target. Edward knew Damon would do anything for his child. And he did.

And here we are.

I step into the aisle and breathe deeply, trying to calm the butterflies in my stomach. Damon is... *gorgeous*. He's as handsome as ever standing at the altar in his tux. His eyes meet mine and something unspoken passes between us. I make my way down the aisle to him, knowing that I've just taken the first steps towards a new life with Damon by my side as my husband.

Damon told me that everyone needs a person, someone who watches and waits to stand guard when life gets all screwed up. He's my person. I know now, more than ever, that he always has been.

*The End*

Turn the page for an exclusive sample of

*Reach* ME

**A Wrecked series companion novel.**
**Coming spring 2014**

# Prologue

---

Journal,

I learned a big lesson today. I learned that a lot can happen in thirty lousy seconds. A half a minute. Apparently that's about how long it takes for some jerk to destroy a girl's self-esteem. I mean, it took a crapload of courage for me to finally talk to him at all. And what did he do? He made me feel like a freakin' joke.

I've had a crush on Jonathan Greene for this whole stupid school year! It's practically the end of sixth grade and it seems like I'm the only girl without a date to the spring dance. I'm not thrilled about going but *not going* just isn't an option. If Sarah Copeland finds out that I don't have a date, she'll tell Katy that none of the boys wanted to ask me. Katy will tell

Shauna because Shauna is new and listens to everything Katy says like she's her mom or something. Then Shauna will blab it to the rest of Harrison Middle School just to strike up conversation with anyone who will listen. Skipping out of the whole thing would suck, but not going would definitely suck more.

So, I waited until Jonathan was done with his lunch tray and I walked over. Thinking about it makes me cringe all over again.

"Ahem. Jonathan?" *Why the heck am I doing this to myself?* I thought my heart would explode any second.

Jonathan was standing by the trashcan looking cute as ever in his Doc Martins and baggy jeans. He turned to face me and I could feel the eyes of the entire sixth grade on me. *Oh God! What am I doing here?*

"Lindsay? What's up?" he said all coolly, which is no surprise. He's the coolest kid in the whole school and I'm no one special. He glanced around us and I did the same only to confirm what I already knew.

Everyone was staring.

*Shoot! Say something, Linds!*

"Ah, well, it's just that you know... the d-dance... and I was just um, you know, wondering if you maybe needed a d-date?" I stuttered out as I shifted from one stupid foot to the other.

"Oh." He looked over at the lunch table that all of his

rotten friends sat at and I could see a couple of the boys snicker and shake their heads. This had bad, bad, bad written all over it. "Nah, no thank you." He smiled his easy smile and walked out of the lunch room just in time for the bell to ring.

My gut turned queasily and I wanted to fake being sick so the nurse would just send me home. *"Nah, no thank you?" What was that?* I offered to go with him to the dance. It wasn't like I offered him the garbage off of my tray!

The buzz of my classmates' giggling as they shoved past me was horrible. I should've listened to Dad. He told me at the beginning of this school year that all boys are punks and to stay the heck away from them. He's right. Guys are nothing but trouble. If I lose my mind and try talking to a boy again, remind me to save myself the trouble and check myself into the nuthouse before the middle school career ending embarrassment happens again, ok?

Thanks,

Lindsay

# Chapter One

---

## 15 YEARS LATER. PRESENT DAY.
## SICKO

There's this state of being called "happiness" and as far as I can tell, it's an illusion. Somewhere deep inside, I guess I associate happiness with magic. There's sleight of the hand and optical illusion, but when it comes right down to it, magic is all about appearance. And so is happiness. Happiness is most definitely an illusion—you think you're happy, that you're doing well... at least from the outside. But on the inside, where it really counts, it's all sleight of hand; you're just showing your audience what they want to see, which is that you *appear* happy. Ergo, happiness=magic.

And let's face the facts on that notion, shall we? I hate to be the bearer of bad news, but there's no such thing as magic. It just doesn't exist. Saying something is magic is just a nice way of admitting you got played. Tricked. Duped. Scammed. Conned. And every time you put on that "happy" façade, you're just playing yourself.

I know this firsthand. I'm no stranger to being conned and everyone in this town knows it. Bottom line: if magic doesn't exist, happiness doesn't exist. For me, at least. I might as well add luck to the list too; I know my maker skipped over me the day he was giving that out.

I have exactly four things going for me. My son, Trey, my dad, and my over-opinionated gay younger brother, Brian. Oh, and, uh, this other... thing. A long-standing relationship with a person I can never have but could quite possibly be utterly and irrevocably in love with. We have this *thing* and it's crazy but we keep coming back to each other. Day after day.

So maybe 3.5 things. I'm not sure this *thing* qualifies, since I don't really know whether it's coming or going.

The thing about having a *thing* is there's always some other *thing* that comes along to muddle it all up. I have these four things and I'm trying damn hard to keep everything headed in the right direction, but it would seem that Central Issue forgot to dole out my flak jacket at the start of this battle called life.

I glance at my cheap wristwatch to check the time. 1:18 p.m. "She's consistent if nothing else," I mutter to myself. I know Maggie will drag herself in any minute. She'll flop into the other side of *our* booth and toss her purse on the table and then she'll start. I should just enjoy the silence while I have it.

My best friend must hold the record for fastest talker on the planet. She rambles on a mile a minute, her junky purse on the table bugs the hell out of me, and her complete lack of punctuality is irritating, but I love her something fierce. She's understanding and supportive and the only person I really have to help with Trey. My younger brother, Brian, helps when he can, but he's almost always tied up doing something for that demanding boss of his.

My tired eyes drift over to the door of the sandwich shop just about the time that Maggie pulls it open. A gust of hot, dry, Las Vegas air comes swooshing in with her and she looks to our booth. I raise a brow and tap my index finger on the scratched up face of my watch.

She looks her typical relaxed self, an eclectic bohemian in strappy gladiator sandals, a coral ribbed tank top, and a long, flowing cotton skirt that seems to have every color of the rainbow sewn into the fabric. Her wavy hair is wild and unkempt and she seems as chill as can be. If I dressed like that, I'd look homeless. Maggie looks like a crunchy hipster gypsy who's just back from following Phish.

"Yeah, yeah. I know," Maggie huffs as she makes the short walk from the door to the first booth that we claimed as "ours" so many years ago. Maggie is the "glass half full" part of this duo and she can keep that title. I'll stick with realism. It's the safest route.

"You know, one day I'm not going to wait and you'll drag in here late and be left to wonder where I went." I smile curtly to cap off my idle threat.

Maggie tosses her purse onto the tabletop right on cue and flops down into the worn, cushy booth. Her long coal black hair drifts easily over her shoulder and I can tell her motormouth is at the ready.

"So?" She leans back passively with questioning eyebrows and I'm honestly shocked.

*One word?* Who is this person and where did my mouthy friend go?! "What?" I ask back as I mirror her relaxed posture.

"You know what! Nick said you never called him. What gives?! Do you want to be some old maid with a dozen cats or something?" she spouts off lightning fast, then takes a hefty draw from the iced tea I ordered when I got here.

"I'm allergic." I dance around the issue at hand, knowing full well that Maggie won't let me skate on this one.

She lets out a low, annoyed growl that seems to emanate from deep in her gut as she drops her head down onto her folded arms. I sit and stare at the top of her head while she mumbles into the small cavern that her arms have made. Her head finally pops up to face me again. "Allergic to what exactly? Happiness? Dating? Casual sex?! Which you need desperately, might I add."

"Hey! Keep it down, loud mouth! I was being a smart ass about the cats. I'm allergic. I don't need casual sex. I manage just fine, thank you very much." I shrug and look down to my lap to avoid Maggie's scrutinizing glare.

"So you finally bought stock in batteries?" she quips with a smirk. One painted plum purple fingertip pops into the air like a loaded weapon and I brace for the zinger. "Oh, I know, you went and got one of those rechargeable ones, huh?! Clever girl," she adds while shaking her head sarcastically. "Going green while getting off. You're a pioneer, my friend. Even better if it's solar powered. Do you set it in the kitchen window to charge? Right next to the basil and dick—I mean dill weed?"

"Hardy har, smartass." I narrow my eyes and nod. "I just haven't had the chance to call him and quite frankly, I'm not chomping at the bit to hook up with him either."

Maggie rolls her wide brown eyes dramatically. She doesn't care about my weak excuse any more than I do. "He's hot. He's a gentleman. He's successful and has no baby mama drama or ex-wives! What's the issue?" she questions as she ticks off Mr. Right's attributes.

"Jonathan. You know they're still friends, right?" I cock an eyebrow at her and watch as she's already begun shaking her head at me.

"Who. Freakin'. Cares? Seriously, doll, you need to get

over the ancient stuff. We were kids. Both times. You're nearing your 30s, chick! Time is running out."

I inhale deeply and decide to do what I always do. Deny. Delay. Deny some more. "Okay, I'll call Nick tomorrow."

"Good!" Maggie chirps victoriously. She smiles widely for only a moment, takes a sip of her drink and looks back at me sympathetically.

*Great.* I love bad news. "No openings, right?" I guess before she does the ugly job of telling me.

"Don't stress about it, okay? Michael said that the minute we're hiring, the first spot is all yours."

I battle against my natural desire to slump in defeat and choke back the disappointment I feel. I'm actually starting to get more frustrated than depressed about my lack of a good job these days. If Maggie pats my hand consolingly, like she usually does, I feel like I might have to slap her. I'm only a temp right now and if I don't find something soon, I'll have no other choice but to get in touch with Trey's father. I hate the thought that I may be forced to swallow my pride and demand that he help with the son he denied so many years ago.

Nine years ago, I was a whopping 19 years old and a freshman at the University of Nevada, Reno. The most complicated thing I had on my plate was figuring out how much slacking I could get away with before I *had* to study for an exam or write a paper.

He was my first love. My first *lover* and my first, and hopefully last, true heartbreak. I fell head over heels in love him. He fell head over heels into my panties a few times and that was that.

He, of course, sent me a ridiculous text message only two months into our relationship that was chock full of bullshit break up lines like, "We're just so different," "It's not you, it's me," and my absolute favorite, "Let's be friends."

I, of course, cried and ate ice cream until I started puking it back up and said to myself, "self, something is not right here."

Two pink lines confirmed what I had already known deep down. I was knocked up, alone, broke, and about to be a college dropout. It took less than a year for me to completely fuck up and lose everything. *Awesome.*

I insisted that Trey's father meet me so that we could talk. I guess I was naïve enough to think that maybe he would make it all right. He didn't. In fact, he didn't even believe me. He said that I was a mistake and he was transferring to a school in Texas to be with his high school sweetheart, Sarah. He said that they were just on a break, whatever the hell that means. I started crying and things quickly went from bad to hellish when he jumped from his seat and spouted off some shit about me lying to him and trying to trap him just like his buddies said I'd do. Needless to say, I bolted from that Starbucks like a woman on fire and never looked back. I'd never felt so cheap and disposable in my life.

I moved back to Vegas and moved in with my dad and younger brother, who were more than supportive. They welcomed Trey into the family like he was the MVP to the Fuller team, helped us out for a few years, and then helped us move on with our lives. Neither of them made a fuss over Trey's father. I told them that I had no interest in going after him for child support and they both respected my decision. Trey and I have been our own little family since the beginning. We don't need the sperm donor. We never have.

I've been too proud to try to find his dad. I never wanted a damn thing from him and I was hoping I never would. I already got the best that he could ever give me anyway. Trey is more perfect than I could ever imagine and it never ceases to amaze me that from that catastrophic "relationship," I came away with this magnificent child.

But now, my temp position is about to end. I've been here for eight months and in one week, I'll be jobless. I have no prospects and no idea how I'm going to pay the bills after that. I dread turning to my father or Brian again; they've already done so much and I want so much to continue to stand on my own two feet, but I only have enough in savings to last us one month. Maybe.

"Earth to Lindsay," Maggie says in her singsong voice.

My attention snaps to her and I shake off my walk down memory lane. There's no use in going there anyway. "Sorry. I was just thinking about some stuff," I mumble as I check my cell phone for the time and secretly hope to see a text message from the one person who might make me forget all about the trouble that awaits me in one short week.

The clock tells me that it's already 2:10 and I have to get my butt over to pick up Trey; my inbox tells me that I do indeed have a text from Russ. *Thank goodness*. My thumb glides over the screen to open the message. I can feel Maggie staring at me. She doesn't approve.

"Still talking to the creeper I see." She leans back and resumes her relaxed posture.

I sigh and smile as I tune out Maggie's diatribe about Russ and read his text.

*Can't wait to talk. Will you be free tonight?*

My thumbs tap out my response and I send the message along.

*Me neither. Bad day. I'll talk to you soon.*

I start gathering my things and look at Maggie. She's shaking her head with this look of part amusement, part skepticism.

"What? He's no creeper! I've known him for nearly ten years, Maggie. I think if he was stalking me so he could rape and murder me, he'd have done it by now." With my eyes averted, I start to gather my things from the seat beside me.

"No. Correction, Linds, you don't know him at all. Russ," she says with disdain. "Who the hell is this guy? Girl? Person?

He could be a psychopath! He could be an old man! He could be *anyone*!"

"Yep. And that's the beauty of it. He could be anyone and it keeps me intrigued," I chime as I scoot out of the booth and smooth my floral print sundress. "Love ya. Gotta run."

"Ugh! Bye, sicko! Only sickos pen pal with strangers for years and years, you know," Maggie bemoans as she stands and only half hugs me goodbye.

I secretly enjoy that my pen pal clearly annoys her, just like her purse on the table annoys the hell out of me.

# About the Author

USA Today Best Selling Author, J.L. Mac, is twenty-seven years old and currently resides in El Paso, Texas, where she enjoys living near her family. She was born and raised in Galveston, Texas. J.L. admittedly has had a long and sordid love affair with the written word and has loved every minute of it. She drinks too many glasses of wine on occasion, and says way too many swear words to be considered "lady-like." J.L. spends her free time reading, writing, and playing with her children.

### Stay connected with J. L. Mac
Twitter: https://twitter.com/JLMacbooks
Facebook: www.facebook.com/jlmacbooks
Blog: http://jlmacbooks.blogspot.com/

### Also by J.L. Mac
*Wreck Me (Wrecked #1)*
*Restore Me (Wrecked #2)*
*Seven Years of Bad Luck*